HIS WORK OF ART

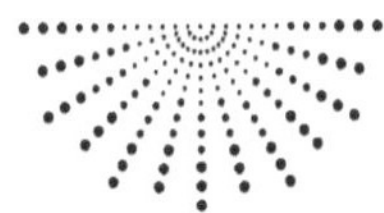

SHANNYN SCHROEDER

DEDICATION

To my nerds – I love you

ACKNOWLEDGMENTS

This second trilogy of Hot & Nerdy novellas was never supposed to be. I wrote the first three and never had any intention of writing more. Then one day, while talking with my daughter about Instagram and whether it was something I needed to do, the idea struck for nerdy guys. Both of my daughters jumped on the concept and filled pages with story ideas for me. While I didn't use many of their notes, they definitely got me moving, so I must thank them for the push. I hope my nerdy guys live up to your expectations. I also need to thank Robyn Bachar for helping me understand tabletop role playing games and answering my silly questions. Any ridiculousness you find is on me. And finally, thank you to my editor, Peter Senftleben, who loved the Hot & Nerdy guys when they were barely a concept.

CHAPTER ONE

*A*dam Hayes stared at the black line drawing and wished for more inspiration. Something was off, but he couldn't quite figure it out. He'd thought that going over the pencil with ink would spark something, but he was still at a loss.

He normally enjoyed days like this at the comics shop. The periodic customer would break the monotony of his frozen brain, but the store was quiet enough that he could get some drawing done.

The masked superhero stared at him. Maybe if it was in color. In Adam's mind, he saw dark skin and darker eyes.

But skin tone and eye color wouldn't give him a name.

The door chimed and Adam looked up to see his friend, Free, walking in. Even from the other side of the store, Adam felt the temperature drop with the blast of cold air that followed Free.

"Hey, man, what's up?" Free called out.

"Nothing." Adam gathered his pages and stacked them on the edge of the table. He walked to the counter to meet Free and took in his appearance. Brown tweed hat and long overcoat. "Meeting Cary at the gym?"

"No, I'm walking around looking like Sherlock Holmes because I thought it would be a good way to pick up a girl."

"It might work. You have a bit of Benedict Cumberbatch going on."

Free threw one of the gloves he'd just removed at Adam. It flopped on the counter.

"Last time I saw Cary he looked good. I thought you were done dressing up to get him through the workouts."

"I probably could be. I think it's mostly habit now. He's come a long way, and I don't want him to lose motivation. Plus, I have an excuse to dress up."

"You say shit like that and then you wonder why chicks think you're gay."

Free rolled his eyes. Adam liked to give him a hard time. For most of his life, Free was a strait-laced banker-in-training, but his love of the theater had allowed him to become anyone he wanted.

Adam envied that skill.

"Where's Hunter? I thought you said three thirty."

"He's late, like always."

The door swung open again and Hunter strode in.

"Why did I have to come here if we're just

talking about the New Year's Eve party? Couldn't we do this at home later?"

"Free has to meet Cary at the gym."

"Then I have rehearsal," Free added.

"Why couldn't it wait? We have like a month before the party." He tucked his hands into the beat-up black leather jacket that he'd been wearing since high school.

Free straightened. "We need to talk about invitations. We don't want a repeat of last year."

"Why not? Last year was epic."

Adam crossed his arms. "Your word-of-mouth campaign led to an apartment full of strangers."

"They weren't all strangers."

"Just the entire marching band."

"Not all of the band came, and it was fun."

"Except for all the drunk bodies laying all over the place the following morning."

Free held up his hands. "I can't say much about that since I don't live with you guys and therefore don't suffer those repercussions, but I agree that it was too crowded to actually have fun with friends."

Adam pointed at Hunter. "And don't forget the catfight that broke out."

"That wasn't my fault. I'm irresistible." Hunter's gaze bounced back and forth between them. "Does that mean you guys are going to have dates this year?"

"Nope," Adam answered. Somehow, he'd always managed to not have a girlfriend over the holidays. It wasn't like he planned it.

Free looked anywhere but at Hunter.

Hunter sighed. "You guys are pitiful. The

epitome of nerds. You get dates, I won't tell everyone and their cousin to come to our party."

"You have a date?" Free asked.

Hunter smiled. "Not yet. I have plenty of time. Working on some options."

Hunter was always investigating his options. The door chimed, and Reese walked through the door with a smile on her face.

"Hi, Reese."

She pulled up short and her eyes widened as she took Adam in, standing with his friends. She took a sharp left and started thumbing through a bin of comics.

Hunter looked at him with eyes almost as wide as Reese's. He then waved a hand toward Reese.

"What?" Adam whispered.

"Ask her, you idiot. She's cute."

"She's not like that."

Hunter shook his head. "Every girl is dateable."

Free checked his watch. "As much as I love your verbal advice column, I have to head out to meet Cary. If I'm not there before him, he might chicken out." He tugged his gloves back on and went to the door. Over his shoulder, he called, "See you later."

Hunter zipped up his jacket. To Adam, he said, "See you at home?"

"Yeah. After closing." He occasionally took the closing shift so his mom could have a free night, and it worked well with his class schedule.

Another customer walked in as Hunter left. Adam was almost able to forget Reese's presence, except now Hunter had put the idea of asking her out in his head. He shoved the thought aside and greeted his customer. "Anything special you're looking for today?"

"My son is eight and I want to get him some comics. But you know, I don't want to spend an arm and a leg because he's eight. He hasn't quite grasped the idea of taking care of his books."

"There are lots of books for kids. We have a clearance section over here." He led the way to the small bin and helped the guy pick out a few comics. Then he went back to his station behind the register to ring him up.

"Wow! You're actually good."

Adam glanced over his shoulder at hearing Reese—words of surprise no guy ever wanted to hear—to see that she stood over his drawing table. Invading his space behind the counter. He thanked the customer in front of him and handed him his bag of comic books. He watched the customer leave before walking up behind Reese.

"Could you—" He gestured to the other side of the counter, the storefront for customers.

She shrugged. "Oh, sorry." She moved to the other side, but continued talking. "It's just that I see you drawing all the time. I wanted to check it out."

Adam moved his panels and sheets of paper back to the order in which he had them. Even if he were to invite her to look at his work, he wouldn't let her shuffle them like a deck of cards. Although she was now standing six feet away, he could still smell her lingering scent. Something soft, but he couldn't quite place it. He found it distracting.

While he continued to straighten his table, he

asked, "Is there something you needed help finding?"

It was a ridiculous question because she was able to find things in the small store as easily as he could. She'd been coming in at least once a week for months, ever since one of their competitors had shut down. Reese had strolled in looking for the latest *Batgirl* comic and his life hadn't been the same since.

"So what are you drawing?"

"Nothing special. Just working up some ideas."

"Those aren't random doodles. I know a superhero when I see one. Who is he?"

Adam set his papers back on the desk. He rubbed the back of his neck, irritation grinding into his muscles. "He doesn't have a name. Not yet anyway."

"He's pretty awesome. You need to name him."

"Yeah, I'll get right on that." As if he hadn't already spent his entire afternoon doing just that. He crossed his arms. "So what are you here for today? You picked up all of your regular issues earlier this week."

"I came to see you." She leaned forward on the counter in front of the register. "I have a proposition for you."

At least these were better words to hear than her first statement. He joined her and braced his palms on the glass and waited.

"I have to do a senior project. My plan is to publish an anthology of comics."

They'd talked about comics plenty over the months. They both had strong opinions, and he enjoyed arguing with her. He also knew that she was a writer, not that he'd ever read any of her stuff.

"And?" he prompted.

"I need an artist. I have most of the stories done." She tilted her head side to side, her straight dark hair swaying with the movement. Squinting her eyes, she said, "Well, they need polishing and maybe some revising, but I figure they'll get fine-tuned as we get to the storyboard phase."

"We?" No way was she asking what he thought.

"If you agree to be my partner, yeah, *we*. I'm under a bit of a time crunch because I have to have things in place to start my crowd-funding campaign. So it'll be a lot of work, but you'll get paid. At least you will if the campaign gets funded. Plus, I figure we have holiday break coming up so we won't have to worry about classes."

"You want me to illustrate your comics?" The thought was a massive blur in his brain. Working together on a comic was intense. He doubted they could get along long enough to complete anything. They managed to argue about just about everything related to comics.

"Yeah. I had the idea a couple of weeks ago when I saw you working at your table. You were so passionate and into it, that it swallowed you. I get like that when I'm in the zone writing. I need that kind of partner." Her stormy blue eyes focused intently on him from beneath her shaggy bangs.

"Do I really need to point out that we don't get along?"

In truth, Reese was one of his all-time favorite customers. She was smart and argued with passion. It was almost enough for him to forgive her for choosing DC over Marvel.

"Who said we have to get along? I'm an excellent writer. From what I can see there, you're an excellent artist. Together, we can put together a fabulous book. " She leaned closer, almost to his side of the counter. "Afraid you can't handle me?"

He chuckled. "Sorry to disappoint, but you don't scare me. However, I don't like to waste my time."

She eased back. "How about this? You can read the story for the first book. Then make your decision. But it'll have to be fast because I have to have everything in place before my campaign goes live. The book doesn't need to be complete, but I have to have enough to entice people to back me."

The idea intrigued him, but Reese would never have been his first choice for a partner. Getting paid to draw was exactly what he was looking for. And if her campaign got fully funded, he would have a publication credit to his name. Having experience like that would help as he started his job hunt after graduation. "Bring it by. I'll take a look."

Her face lit up almost as brightly as when she'd tried to convince him that Batman was better than Iron Man. "Excellent." She reached into her messenger bag and pulled out a purple folder. "Here you go."

He eyed the folder. "You were that sure that I'd say yes?"

She winked at him. "I was cautiously optimistic."

He reached for the folder, but she tugged it back.

"For your eyes only."

The guarded look in her eye made him pause. Who the hell did she think he would show this to? "Got it." He accepted the folder. "When do you need an answer?"

"The sooner the better. I need to get moving."

"Okay. I'll have a decision by next week when you come in for your books."

She pulled a pen from one of the many pockets of her cargo pants, snatched the folder back, and scribbled on the cover. "Here's my number. Call me if you decide before then and we can come up with a plan."

He stared at the number on the folder. "Okay."

"See ya later, Cap'n."

He shot her a dirty look. He hated the nickname she'd given him, Captain. When she first called him Captain, he'd assumed it was after Captain America, but she'd informed him that she went with a DC hero, Captain Atom, whose human last name was Adam. He liked her playfulness, but she could've chosen a cooler hero.

REESE CARTER WALKED CALMLY TO HER CAR, NERVES warming her from the inside out so much that she didn't even notice the wind whipping against her cheeks. Her stomach churned and her hand shook as she opened her car door. She started the engine and sat, settling her nerves and waiting for the car to warm up.

She couldn't believe she'd done it. She'd asked Adam to illustrate her comics. When she'd first walked into Comic Universe months ago, she had just prayed that she wouldn't find an asshole behind the counter who would talk down to her because she had a vagina.

Getting to know Adam had been an unexpected treat. Not only did he never question her choices, except for her love of DC, he also made her feel comfortable in his family's shop. Then last month, she'd seen him at the drawing table, totally immersed in what he was doing.

His hands moved in long, quick strokes, and intense focus filled his face. She hadn't wanted to interrupt him, so she crept close to peek at the drawings. She'd been only able to catch a glimpse, but she knew they were good.

Today was simply a confirmation.

Her phone vibrated in her pocket. A simple text:

I thought you might want my number too. Adam.

The text made her smile and she thanked him before saving his contact information. Then she dialed Julie's number.

"Hello."

"I did it. I talked to Adam and he's got the first book now."

"Adam who?"

"Cute comic shop guy?"

"Oh." Julie stretched the word into four syllables. "So what did he say?"

"He said he'd look at the story and get back to me." She exhaled and could still see her breath. "But I think he's going to do it. I hope he does. He's good."

"I'm glad. When do you think you'll be ready for me?"

"I don't know. It depends on how fast we get moving. After Adam decides and we start work, I'll have a better idea."

"Okay. Meet you after work tonight?"

"Sure." They disconnected and Reese shivered with anticipation. Her project was moving forward. She'd graduate on time.

The heater in her junky car finally rattled to life and the air blew warm. She shifted into reverse to pull out and tried to convince her stomach to settle.

Handing over a not-quite-final draft of her comic worried her. The last time she'd done that, her ideas had been stolen, and she felt so betrayed that she'd stopped writing. Her adviser pointed out repeatedly that part of being a writer meant putting her work out there. Overcoming her fear was a huge part of why she'd chosen this as her senior project.

Getting closer to Adam would be a definite perk.

Over the months, she'd dropped not-so-subtle hints that she'd like to go out with him, but he was either oblivious or uninterested.

She didn't get the impression that he was oblivious.

Trying not to let that last thought get her down, she drove home to change before going to work at the coffee shop. Adam had consented to at least look at her story, which meant that he was agreeable to the idea of working with her. So that was something.

At home, she raced up the stairs to grab her uniform shirt. The atmosphere of Grind was pretty laid-back, which was why she didn't mind working. She could wear jeans or her favorite cargo pants, but she was required to have her hair in a ponytail and wear the brown polo shirt with her name tag.

She'd been working at Grind for three years now, and some of her polos had seen better days. The one she slipped over her head was faded and the color suddenly struck her as the same shade as Adam's skin. Warm and soft, like a teddy bear. She ran her hand to smooth the shirt before pinning her name tag on.

"I thought you already left for work," her mom said from the doorway.

"Uh, no. I had a quick errand to run after class and I forgot to pack my shirt." She gave her mom a quick peck on the cheek and said, "I won't be too late."

Her mom scanned the bedroom and shook her head.

Over her shoulder, Reese called, "I'll clean it later."

But they both knew it was a lie. Ever since she and her mom had moved into their own place ten years ago, Reese hadn't cleaned her room. Well, she'd picked up her dirty laundry and occasionally vacuumed, but her room was never spotless. When they'd moved into the first rinky-dink base-ment one-bedroom apartment, Reese vowed she would live the way she'd wanted to, not how her father had expected.

She swallowed hard. She couldn't afford to

give him any space in her head right now. Her life was heading exactly where she wanted. *Her* life. Independent from everyone.

Her comic book was the first real step. Stories never let her down.

Two days later, Reese had been almost able to put Adam and the fact he had her comic out of her mind. Almost. Then her phone buzzed in her pocket when she was leaving her last class. When she saw Adam's name pop up above the text, her heart crawled into her throat. She stopped and leaned against the wall for support.

I really like this. I have ideas.

Her heart did a weird wobbly thing. He liked it.

But we need her origin.

What do you mean? Her story is explained.

No, we find out she has these powers, but we don't really know how or why. What happened to her when she found out? Why has she been hiding her powers?

Just as her heart settled back into its normal location, her stomach tightened. Adam was not the story guy. He was the picture guy. She didn't need someone to tell her how to write. She knew how to tell a story.

Her story comes out in pieces. A little

throughout the anthology. Otherwise it would be a huge info-dump. No one wants to read someone's life story. They want the story that goes with the comic. Here. Now.

Right after she hit send, her phone rang. She did a double take when it was Adam's name on the screen. "Hello?"

"I hate texting. I don't know why I started that. It's no good when you're trying to talk about a story."

"Okay."

"I see the pieces you've given us in the book. But it doesn't come across as mysterious or engaging. It feels like you're dodging the story. Like you don't want to tell us. Don't you know her story?"

She released a slow breath. "Of course I know her story." And she *was* dodging it a little. It was too personal. Too close to home. "Her origin is too much to be an intro or prologue, but not quite enough for a full issue. I figured my best bet would be to reveal it slowly."

"You're putting together the anthology. Who says the first issue has to be the same length? Make it a mini-issue—*Origins of Lyrid.*"

It was food for thought and echoed what some of her teachers had said about her writing as of late. She didn't go deep enough. Deep was scary.

"You there?"

"Yeah. Just thinking."

"You're kind of light on description too. I don't really know how you see her, so if you could give me something, I can start some rough sketches."

Reese looked around for a place to sit. This definitely wasn't a conversation to have via text.

She was glad he'd called. Nerves still sat on edge, poking her as she sank to a bench near some vending machines. They were going to do this. She had an illustrator for her comics.

"Alexis, the girl, is small, mousy, underdeveloped. She's easily overlooked by everyone around her, like she's invisible."

"That's her character. I get that. What about the obvious—hair color, eye color?"

"Dark hair, black like the night sky. Her eyes are light though. When she's Lyrid, those features stay the same, but she appears a little bigger, stronger. More kick-ass." Reese took a breath. "But maybe not in that first issue. It's like the kick-assery comes from her acceptance of her powers. It takes a while for her to figure them out."

"Maybe she needs a mentor."

Reese had been thinking the same thing. She just hadn't quite figured out how to make one appear. "I know." It seemed like the more she talked about the project, the more changes she wanted to make.

Adam didn't respond. She had no idea where to go from here. "So, uh, did you want me to come by the shop?"

"No. I don't have anything yet. I mean, unless you want to. I don't need you to make a special trip. Hold on a sec."

She heard the cash register dinging in the background. He was working right now. He thanked someone and then to her said, "Sorry about that. Customers tend to come in at the most inopportune times."

"Go figure. They show up when you're open so they can buy comics."

"I know. They get in the way of my conversations."

Reese pictured him sitting behind the counter, his wry smile giving little away. "They should really know better. Almost as bad as all the cranky people I deal with at work. Like I'm the only supplier of caffeine or something."

"Where do you work?"

"A coffee shop called Grind."

"Is it any good?"

"What?"

"The coffee. What else?"

She shrugged before thinking about it. "Maybe you wanted to know if the job was good."

He chuckled, soft and low. The sound tumbled through her and did funny things to her stomach.

"I already have a job," he said.

"I know." She was feeling pretty dumb at the moment. She needed to learn to keep her mouth shut. "Well, I'll let you go."

"Okay. I'll let you know when I have something to show you."

"Thanks." She disconnected and replayed the conversation in her head. Adam had called because he wanted to talk to her. That was a good thing, right? She groaned at herself. She needed to let it go. If the guy was interested, he would've acted already. She needed to focus on her book, her story.

She pushed off the bench and zipped up her jacket before going out in the cold. She jogged across the parking lot and got into her car. After starting the engine, she began to shiver. One day soon, she'd be able to afford a decent car, maybe even have a remote start. Being able to stand inside in the building and warm her car sounded dreamy.

When the heater finally clicked, she put the car in drive and went home. During the drive, all she could think about was what Adam had said about Lyrid's origin story. She knew the story, had it pictured, but could she write it? A huge part of her feared that it wouldn't be interesting enough for a comic.

Lyrid was a superhero—well, at least she was on her way to becoming one. Would readers feel cheated by not knowing where she came from? When she thought about Batman, would she like him less if she didn't know that his parents had been murdered?

She couldn't unknow it, though. The characters' backstory made them who they were. So she was back to square one. She had to decide how much of Alexis and Lyrid she wanted to share with her readers.

Reese ran into her apartment and called out, "Mom?"

No one answered. Strange. Mom wasn't scheduled to work. Maybe she'd picked up an extra shift. As she reached for the refrigerator door, she saw the note:

Hi, Sweetie—working a double shift today, so I probably won't see you. Leftovers in the fridge. Eat some real food, not just cereal. Love, Mom

Reese sighed. Her mom had worked more double shifts than anyone she'd ever met. Every time her mom left her a note like this—and there had been many over the years—Reese felt guilty. Her mom kept pushing her to reach for her dreams. Being a writer was her biggest dream, but she could do something more lucrative. Each of these notes made her question the choice to stick with writing.

She grabbed a Coke from the fridge, ignoring the Tupperware container labeled with directions, and decided to write everything. Lyrid's story might be painful and personal, but she owed it to her mother to write the best damn story possible.

ADAM STACKED REESE'S COMICS AND SLID THEM into a bag. She'd be by today to pick them up, just like every week. He'd had sketches for her comic ready for her days ago, but he couldn't make himself call. Something about needing her approval stopped him. He'd never drawn for anyone but himself, so he was irritated. The questions pounded at his brain for hours on end. What if she didn't like them? What if she laughed? What if she decided this was a huge mistake? The last question was the toughest because he felt invested in this already.

He'd only done the first page of the story in panels because he had to convince Reese to write the origin story. That story would define everything else they did together.

To take his mind off Reese and their comic— when the hell had it become *their* comic?—he unpacked and shelved the rest of the delivery they'd received. Some of his regular customers came in to pick up their orders and he had some other browsers stroll through, but no matter how many people entered the store, all he could do was watch the clock.

Reese always came in after her last class, so depending on traffic, she was normally there by five. In his downtime, he usually sketched, but today he was too antsy. He looked over the drawings he'd made of Alexis and Lyrid. He would need more information in order to complete the book. Reese had been vague about setting and other character descriptions. Getting all of that would probably mean hours more of invested time.

It was a huge undertaking on a possibility of making money.

He reminded himself it wasn't about the money. It was practical experience working with a writer. The project would give him complete panels for his portfolio when he hit the conventions in the spring.

It was all very practical. Spending time with Reese had nothing to do with it. At least that's what he kept telling himself.

When she finally came barreling through the door, he'd almost convinced himself of all of his rationalizations. Her cheeks were pink from the cold and she wore a bright smile. "Hey."

"Hi. I've got your stuff all bagged up already." He slid the plastic bag onto the counter.

"Trying to get rid of me?"

"No," he answered too quickly and then realized he probably sounded like an idiot. "I have some drawings for you."

Her face lit with excitement, which added more pressure to what he already felt.

"Let me see. Let me see." She reached out with grabby hands.

He walked to his drawing table and picked up the sheets. "Before you get too excited, they're only pencil. I haven't inked anything since we didn't talk about colors and stuff."

Her hand snapped up to cut him off. "Wait. You can color too?"

"Yeah, but I didn't because I didn't want to impose my ideas onto you."

"Really?" She crossed her arms. "Like telling me that I *had* to write a full origin story wasn't imposing your ideas?"

He gripped the pages tighter and then forced his fingers to relax. He had to get used to working with other people if this was the career he wanted. "Okay, yeah, I was, but you know I'm right."

She dropped her arms. "You totally are. I'm almost done with it."

"Yeah?"

"I thought about what you said and thought about Alexis, and when I sat down to write, it just came to me." She reached out again. "Now show me."

He handed her the pages and curled his fingers into fists to prevent himself from snatching them back.

"Oh my God."

He had no idea how to interpret that, so he waited for more to go on. She hadn't even gotten past the top page.

She looked up at him with teary eyes.

Crap. He'd never made a girl cry before. "I'm sorry?"

She took a swipe at his shoulder. "What are you apologizing for?"

"You look like you're about to cry."

"First, happy tears. This is exactly how I pictured Alexis. You completely nailed it. Second, if that was supposed to be a real apology, it sucked. You asked. It's not a question."

He shrugged. "I didn't know if I was supposed to be sorry for something. This is the first time I've worked with someone else's ideas."

"I never would've guessed. She's perfect." She traced a finger over the drawing before flipping to the next page. She snickered. "You're kidding, right?"

"What?"

"Now you do owe me an apology."

"For what?"

She spun the drawing of Lyrid around to face him as though he didn't know what he'd drawn.

"Seriously?"

"What's wrong?" he asked cautiously.

"Look at her." Then she held the page of Alexis beside the one of Lyrid.

"You said that you wanted Lyrid to be bigger and stronger."

"I meant muscular. Not titty heaven. She's nothing but boobs. And they're popping out everywhere."

Adam opened his mouth, stopped, closed it, and waited. He wasn't sure what he was supposed to say. He thought Lyrid looked pretty kick-ass, which was what Reese had requested.

Reese's eyes about popped from her skull as she grunted and slapped the pages on his desk. Then she spun and headed for the door. She seemed really pissed.

"Wait!"

She stopped but didn't turn around. The rise and fall of her shoulders told him her breathing was fast and she was far from calm. He walked toward her holding three comics, making sure the ones he chose were all DC so she had little argument about his preferences. He lined them up on the bins of comics for sale.

"I wasn't trying to offend you. Like it or not, it's how female superheroes are drawn." He pointed to the comics. "Look at some of your favorites: Wonder Woman, Black Canary, Huntress. In addition to being kick-ass heroines, they have sexy bodies. There's no denying that."

Reese stared at the covers of the comics. He shrugged. "I drew what I'm familiar with. It's not like you gave me much to go on. These are first sketches, ideas. We can work from here."

She inhaled deeply and closed her eyes. He waited, unsure if he was supposed to say something.

When she reopened her eyes, she looked at him. "You're right. It is standard, but that doesn't mean I have to like it. Lyrid is not a sex object."

"I wasn't suggesting she is."

Reese's eyebrows disappeared behind her bangs. "But you drew her like every man's fantasy."

"Not every man's." As soon as the words left his lips he wished they hadn't. While he could appreciate a huge rack on a superheroine, it wasn't his thing. But he didn't really want Reese to question what his thing was. He waved his hand as if to erase what he'd said. "I drew her in the vein of other comics. It's open for revision. However, that's what sells."

Reese's shoulders dropped. "But I want to be different," she said quietly.

"So let's talk about what you want. What you expect. You said I nailed Alexis. Doesn't that show I can handle this?"

She nodded. "When do you have some free time to meet and talk about it?"

"I'm free now."

She looked around the shop. "I know this place isn't fighting off customers or anything, but aren't you at work?"

"My mom owns the place. We can order pizza and work here if it suits you."

Her easy smile came back. "If you're sure it's okay."

He scooped up the comics he'd laid out and headed back behind the counter. He'd successfully talked his way into a partnership with a writer. Now all they had to do was learn to listen to each other.

CHAPTER THREE

By the time the pizza arrived, Reese's stomach was growling loud enough for Adam to be staring at her. They left their work on his drawing desk and took the pizza to a small table behind the counter. Adam flipped up the lid on the box, and the steamy smell of gooey pizza hit her. She shouldn't have skipped lunch.

She reached for a slice as Adam walked in the back. He returned with some napkins, which was good because she now had sauce dripping on her chin. "Thanks," she mumbled around a mouthful of hot cheese. Just as she wiped at her chin, a blob of sauce landed on her cargo pants. She rubbed at it, resigned to another stain.

The corners of his mouth lifted, but he said nothing. He leaned against the counter in front of the register. They ate in silence through their first pieces. They'd worked a long time to figure out how to approach this partnership.

No matter what, collaboration was rough.

Adam wiped his hands on a napkin. "Do you think this is going to work?"

"What? Us?" Probably not the best wording. He nodded.

"As long as you give up your boob fixation, yeah." She blew out a heavy breath that puffed her bangs away from her forehead. "It's harder than I thought. It'd be cool if we could just do a Vulcan mind meld, and you could see inside my head and know what I'm picturing. If I had any artistic skill, I'd attempt to draw it myself. But I find stick figures challenging."

"So Lyrid can't have big tits. I get it. You can stop telling me. But I'm not going to draw her like a guy either."

The jab hit home. More times than she cared to think about, people had commented on her appearance. "I don't want her to be a guy. But real women don't have a two-inch waist to go with their ginormous boobs."

"Lyrid isn't real. She's a character. A fantasy."

But why did the fantasy always have to be sex goddess? "Can we settle on a happy medium?" She squinted at him and searched for the right words. "Curvy, but not voluptuous?" She pointed at him. "And no spillage."

"Spillage?"

She cupped her hands in front of her own small chest. "Spillage. Popping out of a ridiculous outfit."

Adam dropped his pizza back in the box and went to the drawing table. He flipped up his sketch pad. An intense expression took over his face and Reese stared. She couldn't look away. His long fingers moved quickly with a pencil in his left hand. She knew that when he was finished, smudges would be smeared on the edge of his palm as well as on his fingertips.

It was like she was no longer in the room. The bell over the door jingled as a customer came in. Adam's shoulders tensed, but he didn't look up. He definitely didn't like to be interrupted. Reese quickly wiped her hands clean and walked around the counter. "Hi, can I help you find something today?"

Adam shot her a look like she'd lost her mind, but she continued.

The customer, a guy about her age, lifted a shoulder. He didn't appear any more convinced than Adam was that she could take care of a customer. "Nah. Just looking."

"Okay. Let me know if you need any help." She hung back, still in the aisles to make herself available. She tried her best to ignore Adam's presence.

The guy looked up from a bin of comics. "Do you have the latest *Amazing Spider-Man*?"

She wanted to glance back at Adam to check, but she also didn't want to interrupt him. Seeing his new sketch of Lyrid was exciting. "I believe it came in today's shipment. Let me check."

She went to the bin where the comic should be located. Sure enough, there it was. "Did you need anything else?"

"Yeah, I need some more plastic covers for my collection."

Reese wove around to the other side of the store and grabbed a packet of sleeves for him. "Just one pack?"

"That'll do."

She walked back to the counter to ring him up, but Adam was already standing behind the register. She laid the purchases on the glass and let Adam take over. She returned to the pizza, which was now cold.

When the customer left, Adam stood by her side and bumped her shoulder with his. This was the closest they'd been and she liked it. "Trying to steal my job? I told you my mom owns the shop. I doubt she'd choose you over me."

"Funny. I was being helpful. I want to see the new Lyrid."

He stretched across to the other side of the register, where he'd tossed his sketch pad. "Here."

Before taking the pad from him, she wiped her hands on her pants and took a deep breath. If this was still wrong, their partnership might not work. How many times would they want to go back and forth? She held her breath and flipped the pad over.

The sketch was rough, with smudges and eraser marks, but it was better. Lyrid's boobs were still a little on the big side and her waist too small, but she looked a little sturdier. Less like a model in a mask and more like a fighter.

"Let me guess—smaller chest?"

"No, well, yeah, if I had my choice, it might be, but you have a point. If I want everyone to be willing to buy, I have to appeal to all kinds of readers, including men." She studied the drawing. "Can we make her costume not a bustier? But I like her arms showing. Great muscles."

Adam took the pad back, swiftly erased some lines, and shaded in a vest.

"That's good. I like it."

"You don't sound sure."

Was she? This was so new. Why the hell didn't she just decide to write a book or something for her project instead of this huge undertaking? Because this was what she wanted in life. She wanted to write comics. She wanted to represent the millions of girls like her who wanted heroes and heroines that were like them.

"I'm sure. I think."

"Revisions are still possible. I have lots of erasers."

Even if the sketch wasn't the right one, she'd definitely chosen the right partner. She needed to take lessons from him on flexibility. "Tell me about your superhero guy. The one I saw last week."

"What do you want to know?"

"What's his story?"

"I'm an artist, not a writer. He doesn't have a story."

"Everyone has a story. You have one. I have one. It colors everything we do and see and say. There's a piece of us in everything we create." She handed him the pad back and began to clean up their dinner mess. "Tell me something about him."

"He's not white."

ADAM HATED THAT THE FIRST COMMENT HE MADE

was about race. Reese turned and leaned against the table she'd just cleared of their dinner. She pursed her lips before speaking. "So race is important."

"Yeah. There aren't enough people of color in comics." The statement was true, but not the reason.

"Not enough, no. But we have Green Lantern and Cyborg."

This was solid footing for them, arguing the merits of comics. "Marvel has Black Panther. And let's not forget the new Ms. Marvel, who is a double whammy as a woman and a person of color."

"If you think you're going to convince me Marvel is better based on this argument, you're out of luck. I get the importance of full representation. I *am* a woman. That's why the portrayal of Lyrid is so important. So your guy, he's black?"

"Yeah."

"I guess what I'm really asking is if he's black just because that's how you envision him or if you made him black because it's part of your character building."

And there went the footing. "You can't take race away from character. It's part of who you are."

"It doesn't have to be."

He snorted. "Only naïve white people say shit like that."

"Hey." She stepped toe to toe with him, tilting her chin a notch. Irritation blazed from her blue-gray eyes. "I am not naïve. I believe race is only as important as you make it in your life."

He wanted to cross his arms, needed to, but the

action would make him come in contact with her. She was close enough that the movement would cause his forearms to brush her chest. That couldn't lead to anything good. "You have no idea what you're talking about. No one considers your race first because you're white. Everyone considers my race first because I'm not."

"Not everyone." A flash of hurt crossed her face, quickly replaced by anger. "But people do look at my gender first. Mostly men, but it's the same idea. They don't consider whether I'm intelligent or kind. They want to see how big my boobs are, how thin my waist is, how shapely my ass is. The quality of the rest of me is shaded by that." As she spoke, her hands waved out at the sides of her body emphasizing everything she said.

Those motions almost distracted him. She had a point, but he didn't want to have this discussion with her. He didn't want to have it with anyone. There was no way she could ever fully understand.

She stopped moving. "I don't let that run my life. It mostly doesn't even take up space in my head. Only when I'm faced with something like a guy in a comic shop who assumes I'm buying for my boyfriend."

"I never did that."

"No, not you, which is why I spend my money here. My point is, I don't walk through life worrying about how other people view me. I just try to be the best I can for me."

Adam tried to do the same, but it didn't always work. He took a step back. "All I'm saying is that my guy is black. I picture him that way, but it's also who he is. His race colors his perception of things."

She inched closer again. "Why?"

"What do you mean, why?"

"That's his story. That's the part you're telling me doesn't exist, but it does. You know it, in here." She poked his chest.

His heart thumped so hard he was sure he'd need CPR any minute. Why couldn't she take a hint? As much as he wanted to step back again, he also wanted to step forward. But he knew better.

Reese took mercy on him and stepped away. She walked over to the table and flipped through his sketch pad. She found a picture of the character they were discussing. "I want his story. Even if we don't make it a book, I want to know."

The way she looked into his eyes stirred something in Adam, but he didn't know quite what. It was like she was asking for much more than a character's history. Adam tore away from the staring contest that pulled at him. "So, write it," he mumbled.

"I can't write his story. He's not mine."

Adam reached over, took the book from her hand, and ripped out the page. "Here. Now he's yours."

Although she accepted the paper, she rolled her eyes. "Fine. I'll create a story for him, and then I'll kill him off." She smirked as she tucked the page into her bag in between books.

"You can't kill my character."

"He's mine now. You gave him to me, so I can do whatever I want."

"You sound like a little kid."

"I need to get home. You have enough to start working on panels now? If we can get the pencil drawings done, that would be great. I should have the origin story finished in a couple days." As she spoke, she put away the folder that she'd brought out. She faced her bag the whole time she talked. "Are you free at all this weekend?"

"Saturdays are pretty busy around here, so that probably won't work."

"How about Saturday night after you close?" She slung her bag over her shoulder and turned.

"Sure. Where do you want to meet? My roommate's a musician, so my place is usually loud."

"Noise doesn't bother me."

"Wish I could say the same."

"My roommate's my mom, but she works weird hours. Even if she is home, she'll probably be asleep or whatever." She hitched the bag higher on her shoulder. "We could meet at a library or something, but it's always too quiet there."

"If you don't mind me coming to your place, I'm cool with that."

"Sure." Pulling a pen from a thigh pocket, she wrote her address on a napkin leftover from their dinner. "I'll be home all night, so come by whenever. I have a paper to write, so I'll be chained to my computer."

"Paper on what?"

"Anything. It's such a pain in the ass. This professor thinks she's cool by leaving everything open-ended. The only direction we have is that we have to write a critical analysis of something."

"So write about something you care about.

Like why people got so upset when Marvel revealed a female Thor."

"First, stop trying to sell me on Marvel. Second, no analysis needed there. People are dumb."

"You want to talk about dumb, should we discuss some movies made about DC characters?"

She groaned. "No. Their movies are improving. I could do Batman."

It was his turn to groan. "The idea of college is to broaden your horizons and learn something. If you write about Batman, you'll get bored. You know it all."

"At this point in my academic career, I'm looking for easy. I'm ready to be done."

He was well acquainted with that feeling. "How about an analysis of the mythology of Thor? It would give you an excuse to sit and watch movies by calling it research."

He knew she liked the idea because something lit in her eyes.

"I'll even bring my copy on Saturday. You do your research between now and then and you can compare it to the movie. Still easy." It'd be nice if someone came along with ideas for him whenever he faced a school project.

"We'll see. But I'll have your story done—your superhero's story. You sure you don't want to at least give this guy a name?" Her cocky smile returned and she had a scheming look in her eye.

"Nope. I trust you. As long as you don't kill him."

"Fine. But torture is totally still on the table." She grabbed her jacket off the chair and headed for the door. "See you Saturday."

Adam stared after her for a while, unsure of what he'd gotten himself into. Hanging out at her apartment, working, watching a movie. He hoped she didn't get the impression this would be a date. He didn't need that kind of complication as they headed into this partnership. Plus, as much as he liked Reese, she was all wrong for him.

CHAPTER FOUR

Reese was nervous about Adam coming over. She'd had plenty of friends at her apartment over the years, both guys and girls. She'd even had boyfriends spend the night. But having Adam in her home was strange. Their relationship was so undefined. Were they friends? Partners? He was right when he'd pointed out that they had a hard time getting along, but even their disagreements were fun.

Having him here would change who they were. He would know more about her than she knew about him. She didn't like that. He texted that he'd be there around eight and offered to bring dinner. He'd supply the burgers and she had the beer. She also had plenty of junk food to fuel their creativity for the night.

She had roughly five weeks before she launched her campaign. By that time, she needed to have at least part of the anthology done; illustrations would make the sales. Take out a few days for the holidays, and they would have maybe a month of work time and both she and Adam still had classes.

Depending on how well tonight went, they might just be able to pull some late nights to get things moving. She tossed a blanket over the couch to cover the worst of its age. When the doorbell rang, she took one last look around to make sure she hadn't left her underwear on the floor, or anything equally embarrassing, then ran down the stairs to let Adam in.

She swung the door open and said, "Sorry. The buzzer's broken. I'm upstairs." She turned and led the way back into her apartment.

Adam followed her through and set the bag of food on the coffee table. She locked up and asked, "You want a beer or pop?"

"Whatever you're having." He shucked his jacket and hung it on the overloaded coatrack. "You want me to take my shoes off?"

"Doesn't matter. I like to be barefoot, but it's not a requirement." She snagged two bottles of beer from the fridge and joined him at the couch.

Adam unpacked the food and asked, "How much did you get done this week?"

"Story?"

He nodded. "Or paper."

"Lyrid's origin is done, but not broken into panels. I'm finding that's hard to do. Trying to find the right place to break things, how much to fit in each panel, deciding which panels should be bigger because they're more involved." She sat on the floor and crossed her legs. "Your story is done, too."

"My story?"

"Your superhero. I still don't have a name, but I'm working on it. You'd be surprised how many names are already used in comics. Everything I came up with I had to toss because Marvel or DC had already used it. That doesn't even touch the smaller pubs like Dark Horse. Google was not kind to me this week."

Adam settled back on the couch with a burger in his lap and said nothing. So she continued, "His is a story of redemption. He's badass, a felon, always in trouble. Then, one night, he does the unthinkable. He gets his girlfriend killed." She bit into her burger and let Adam digest that part of the story.

"Ouch." Adam narrowed his eyes as he took another bite. "But I like an anti-hero."

"Totally!" She took another hasty bite and continued, "So while he's in prison, he saves some dude's ass—literally and figuratively. And he likes it. He starts to think that if he does enough acts like that, he can make up for all the bad he's done. When he gets out, he takes a menial job, because how many choices does a guy like him have? Whatever that job is, it puts him on the streets where he can help people."

"That sounds way more superhero than anti-hero."

"It's a work in progress. The anti-hero part is that he's not doing this for other people, he's all about saving himself, which means he spends a lot of time being an asshole to everyone." She took a pull on her beer to wash down the food.

Adam laughed. "You sound like you're getting off on him being an asshole."

She snorted and beer bubbled up her nose. Crap. *Real sexy, Reese.* She coughed to cover how much that hurt as she wiped a napkin over her face.

Adam stood. "Are you okay?"

She nodded and waved him off. He returned to his seat and finished his food while she attempted to regain her composure. When she was able to breathe normally and her nose burned only a little, she went back to her dinner. "I don't get off on him being an asshole. I just think it makes for a deep and intriguing character."

He laughed. At her. "It's okay, Reese. Call it whatever you want. You like bad boys. You wouldn't be the first girl."

She whipped a French fry at him. He picked it up and ate it.

"On that note, I want to use him. Don't you think he'd make a great mentor for Lyrid?"

"What?"

"Think about it. They're both reluctant heroes. He thinks he has to be one to clean the slate. She's afraid to be one."

"He'll feel the need to protect her like he couldn't his girlfriend."

Reese stood. "See, you are good at story. You just need a little prompting." She gathered all their trash and tossed it in the kitchen.

By the time she returned to the living room, Adam had the table wiped off and their bottles moved to the side table. He had pages spread out, but they were all blank.

"I thought you were going to have drawings."

"I will. I'm fast. At least the first sketches. I

need to see the story, to know the layout. That's stuff we need to do together. Unless you're leaving all of that to my judgment."

Hell no. She grabbed the notebook that contained her stories and knelt next to him at the table. "Here's her origin."

She laid the notebook down and then scooted back to sit on the couch while he read.

"You actually write on paper? I thought everyone used computers."

"Paper doesn't lose battery power. It doesn't crash or accidentally erase. You work on paper."

"I like the feel of it."

"So do I. If my writing's too hard to decipher, I can type it up. It wouldn't take long."

"You're fine." He spoke softly because he was already reading.

This was harder than just handing over a folder of her work. This was even harder than having to read a sample aloud in class. She gulped the rest of her beer and went to the kitchen to grab another. She came back and Adam had abandoned the notebook and was already scribbling on his sheets.

She knelt next to him, her freshly opened beer forgotten. He scribbled in the boxes of the panels, outlining the story. His drawings were placeholders, little more than blobs and sticks. She could've done that. He said nothing, but continued to scratch through one page after another, occasionally referring back to her notebook.

As he finished a page, she took it and outlined where the text boxes and speech bubbles would go. It started to take shape, like a real book. When he had five pages done, he stopped and looked at what she'd done on the first three.

"What do you think?"

She eyed the last two pages. "That's not the end."

"Nope. I think we can turn this origin story into a full book, not a mini-book."

"But there's not a whole lot of action to show. No one wants to read big blocks of text."

"There's enough to look at. Trust me. But this"—he tapped page three—"I think this one needs to be a full page. Getting struck by the power of what she thinks is a shooting star changes the entire course of her life."

Reese looked at the panels. "If we juggle these," she said, pointing to the small panels on the top of the page, "stretch them to be three long panels instead of boxes, then the next page will be the big splash."

Adam dug through his pile of papers for a new sheet, this one with the panels as she described. How much did this guy spend on copying panel pages? He came prepared with everything.

As Adam laid out more blank pages, he was in the zone. This was real creation. What he expected when creating a real story. Until now, he'd never experienced this kind of collaboration. Bouncing ideas off Reese was so much better than trying to talk to Hunter, who just didn't get comics. For over an hour they worked, arguing over layout and important plot points. But in the back of his mind, he knew there was something special about this story. The origin of Lyrid was personal for Reese.

She scribbled quick lines of dialogue and description on the pages he'd already sketched and he glanced at her from the corner of his eye. The pain she described of Alexis's home life, living with an abusive father, made Adam wonder. He looked around the small apartment. He saw no sign of any man, but that didn't have to mean anything.

With the exception of things he'd left at his mom's house, there was no sign of a man there either and his father hadn't been abusive. He returned his focus to the remaining pages in front of him. Rough sketches that wouldn't mean much to anyone stared back at him. This was a huge undertaking.

Part of him worried he wouldn't be up to the challenge. On the other hand, they'd just managed to draft an entire comic in one night. They could do this. He sat back on the couch and drank from a glass of water that Reese had brought in for him. He waited while she finished off the text. "I brought *Thor.*"

At first he wasn't sure if he'd said it out loud because she didn't respond. He'd debated for a long time before leaving his apartment about whether he should bring the disc. She hadn't asked him to and he didn't even know at this point what her paper was about, but he wanted to share something he liked with her.

She finally looked up from the page. "Thanks."

She glanced down again and then asked, "Did you want to stay to watch it?"

"Sure." Adam dug in his bag to grab the box. "I'm not trying to strong-arm you into watching a Marvel movie. If you decided on something else for your paper, we don't have to."

She looked up again and her cool eyes met his. "Contrary to what you think, I don't hate Marvel. I've seen some of the movies. I really liked *Guardians of the Galaxy*."

"I am Groot." He couldn't help it. Three words ended up defining the movie. He walked over to the DVD player and inserted the disc. "I assume you took note of all of the kick-ass women in that movie. Marvel is flush with them."

"Yeah, yeah. We have a Wonder Woman movie."

"I'm surprised they didn't screw it up."

As Reese dealt with the remote to get the movie started, Adam cleaned up their work. "Do you want me to start inking these when I have them ready, or do you want to see them first?"

She scrunched up her whole face. "I think I want to see them, if you don't mind. It's not that I don't trust you. I just…"

"Want to make sure I don't screw it up?"

"Yeah. I mean, no offense, but this is my grade we're talking about. If it's still in pencil, we can make changes, right?" The previews blared to life on the TV screen as she settled on the opposite end of the couch.

"It's fine, Reese. I get it. You want majority control."

"I didn't say that."

"Okay, you just want final say." At this point, he was just poking at her because it was fun, but she didn't seem to get it.

Her face scrunched up again. Then a look of defiance came into her eyes. "Yeah, actually, I do. I might not be able to draw for shit, but I have a vision of what I want the books to be."

Adam laughed, which seemed to frustrate her even more. He waved a hand. "I'm fucking with you. We both need to accept that there are things we'll go to bat for in our work. We didn't have any problems tonight, and we got the first book done. I'm not concerned with your final say."

She shot him another dirty look. She should learn that doing that only made her look sexy, not mean. Reese returned her attention to the remote and went to the main menu. As the opening credits rolled, she pulled out a notebook and pen.

"Taking notes?"

"I need to have specifics for my paper." She brought her legs up onto the couch and crossed them with the notebook balanced on her knee.

"Wait. Did she just hit Thor with her car?"

Adam held up a hand. "This is like a prologue. It'll go back and you'll understand everything. Be patient."

About halfway through, Reese paused the movie, and said, "I don't get it. I've heard so many people talk about Loki. Where's the love coming from? I don't like him. He's a weasel. As a character, he's complex and has great motivation, but I don't think I'll ever be rooting for him."

"Maybe they're just crushing on Tom Hiddleston."

"You might be on to something there." She slapped his leg. "I'm hungry. It doesn't seem right to be watching a movie without popcorn. You want some?"

"Sure."

She stood and stretched, going all the way on tiptoe and reaching her arms above her head. Her shirt rose, revealing smooth skin on her waist and before he could avert his eyes, she bent over and slapped her hands on the floor. The girl was damn flexible.

On her way into the kitchen, she turned off the overhead light. The room wasn't plunged into darkness because of the glow from the kitchen, but Adam felt a little uncomfortable. That was the kind of move he'd make if he were on a date. Was that what she thought this was?

Adam wrestled with how to tell her that he didn't want this to be a date. Dating would definitely mess up their new partnership. Which would ruin her project and her grade. Definitely better to keep it platonic. Plus, he knew that relationships between people with their differences had a shaky record at best.

But when she came back into the room, she carried two bowls of popcorn and a couple cans of pop. No romantic sharing of food. He'd misread the situation. He mentally slapped himself and stood to help her.

They returned to their respective spots on the couch and Reese restarted the movie without saying anything.

Adam settled back into the comfort of the film and forgot about what he'd believed was Reese flirting with him. Yeah, she was cute, but he saw cute girls all the time. He didn't walk around thinking they were all hitting on him. Reese was being friendly.

Near the end of the movie, a *thump* sounded at the door, and as Reese moved to stand, it swung open. It had to be Reese's mom because they looked a lot alike. The woman was older and wore hospital scrubs. Her dark hair was pulled back into a ponytail and she looked exhausted. "Christ, Reese, I keep telling you to leave a light on for me so I don't trip over any of your crap."

Shifting the bag she had in one hand, she slapped against the wall and flooded the room with bright light. Adam squinted.

Reese paused the movie again. "Hey, Mom." She stood and pointed at Adam. "This is Adam. He came over to work on my comic. Adam, this is my mom, Linda."

He bristled a little at the reference to the comic being *hers*. At this point, it was definitely *theirs*.

"Oh" was the only response her mother made.

Adam knew that look. In spite of it, he stood to shake her hand. "It's nice to meet you."

"You too." She shook his hand and forced a tight smile.

At least she didn't look afraid or disgusted. In the past, those were emotions he'd witnessed. It was like *Uh-oh. A black man is in my living room.*

Adam edged away. Linda dropped her bag on the table across the room and disappeared around the corner, closing a door behind her.

"I should probably be leaving."

"What? The movie's almost over."

He looked across the room to where her mom had walked.

Reese waved a hand. "She's going to take a shower and then probably crash. She just worked a double shift."

"Is she a nurse?"

"CNA. They had a bunch of cutbacks at the hospital and the only way for her to keep her job is to work like two people."

"That sucks." He grabbed his bag and made sure everything he needed for the comic was there.

"Seriously. You can stay. She doesn't care."

He set his bag at his feet. "She looked like she cared. And if she's tired, she doesn't want a stranger in her house while she's trying to sleep."

Reese laughed. "My mom doesn't mind. She sleeps through everything. Come on. Let's finish. You can help me with your witty commentary."

He stared at her for a minute. She really had no idea that her mom was uncomfortable. Could she be that clueless? He thought back to their conversation about race and knew that, yeah, she kind of was that clueless. She grabbed his arm and shoved him back toward the couch.

She started the movie again with a smile on her face. He sat and half-focused on the TV. Part of his brain cued in on the sounds behind him: doors opening and closing, water running, quiet music.

By the time the credits hit the screen, he was exhausted. He stood and stretched. "Did you get enough for your paper?"

"Yeah, I think so. This was a good idea. Do you

mind if I keep the movie in case I want to rewatch to fill in stuff?"

"No problem."

"I'll bring it in on Wednesday when I stop by to get my order."

"No hurry."

He pulled on his coat and swung his bag on his shoulder.

"When do you think you'll have those pages done so we can talk about inking them?" She followed him to the door with her hands shoved in her pants pockets.

"We have a really big shipment Wednesday, so I'll probably be pulling orders all day. How's Thursday?"

"No good for me." She bit her lip. "Friday night? I'm off work at seven."

"Okay. You just want me to bring your books then?"

"Heck, no. I want to gobble them up as soon as they come in. I'll be there as usual on Wednesday."

"Same Bat-time, same Bat-channel?"

"You know it."

Adam walked out of her apartment and breathed in a lungful of cold air. Everything about Reese unsettled him, and he needed to get it under control. He needed to focus on finishing school and getting work. He didn't have time to start any relationship, much less a complicated one.

CHAPTER FIVE

Adam worked on little sleep for days. When he wasn't in class, he was driven to draw Lyrid's story. By Wednesday morning, he was ready to mainline coffee. As much as he wanted to stay in bed, he couldn't because his mom needed help with the delivery and pull lists like she did every week. At some point, they would have to hire a replacement for him; he had no intention of continuing to help his mom run the store after graduation.

With any luck, this would be his last winter in Chicago. Even if he didn't get his dream job at Marvel in California, he'd move wherever he had to in order to illustrate comics. He sat at the kitchen table and gulped coffee. Hunter walked in wearing only his boxers.

"Aren't you cold?" Adam huddled over the steam from his cup.

"Nope." He reached in the cabinet for a box of cereal. He shoved his hand in and when he pulled out a fistful of flakes, more scattered on the floor.

"Shit." He pushed the flakes in in his mouth before bending over to pick up the mess.

That was Hunter. Man of few words. Unless a woman was involved. Then he always had plenty to say. When he straightened and dumped the crumbs in the trash, he looked at Adam. "I've barely seen you for days. What the hell has you so busy?"

"A project."

"Figures."

"What's that supposed to mean?"

"When you go with no sleep for days, it's supposed to be because you're fucking your brains out and you have all the energy in the world. This"—he pointed at Adam—"is sad."

"Some of us have bigger goals than to play music and get laid."

"Those aren't my only goals." He smirked. "Just my primary ones." He plopped on the chair across from Adam, laying the box of cereal on its side in front of him. "So what's the project?"

"This girl I know, Reese, is trying to publish an anthology of comics as her senior project. She asked me to illustrate for her."

"So it is a woman keeping you up."

"Not like that."

"Only because you're lame. Why the hell would you do that much work if you're not getting laid?"

"It'll be a publishing credit and if it sells, I'll make money. It'll also look good in my portfolio when I search for a job." He finished his coffee and refilled the cup. If he drank fast, he could finish it before heading to the store and the caffeine might be just enough.

"Sometimes it's good to step back and not be so driven."

"Says the king slacker."

Hunter shook his head. "Do you have a date for the party yet?"

"I told you I probably wouldn't. Between school and work, where do I have time to meet anyone?"

"Yeah, the work situation sucks. Hard to meet beautiful women when you're surrounded by geeks and loners."

But he'd met Reese at the shop. Adam almost opened his mouth to say that to Hunter but caught the mistake before letting loose. As much as he wanted to prove Hunter wrong about the quality of their customers, he didn't want to invite him to ask about Reese.

"Why don't you come by the bar on Friday? I'll hook you up with some chicks."

The thought of who Hunter might find for him was a little frightening. "Sorry. Busy Friday night."

"Busy with what?"

"Working on the comics." He stood and dumped his cup in the sink. Under his feet, cereal flakes crunched into dust. "Sweep the damn floor. This is gross."

"Whatever. Ask your comic lover if she has a friend. Someone needs to find you a date."

Adam left the room without answering. He didn't need anyone, Hunter or Reese, to find him a date. From his room, he heard Hunter yell, "We had a deal. No date means I start making calls to fill the apartment with strangers. Maybe a flyer up at the bar."

Crap. That sounded exactly like something Hunter would do. Adam wouldn't care if Hunter invited people from the jazz club he worked at a few nights a month, but he was talking about a flyer at the grunge bar where he regularly worked.

Their New Year's Eve party had begun four years ago, when they got their first apartment together. Adam longed to go back to those days. A few friends, some drinks, Hunter playing music. Last year, their party could've rivaled a rave. If he wanted to prevent that from happening, he needed to prove to Hunter that he could get his own date.

HOURS LATER, ADAM'S BACK WAS KILLING HIM AS HE hauled another box to the front of the store to pull orders while manning the register. His mom had opened the store that morning and received the inventory. Now she was off doing whatever business stuff he knew she did, but didn't care enough about to learn the specifics. He filled the pull lists, happy to note there were three new ones this week.

Their customer base was growing, which eased his worry about his mom. He'd saved Reese's order for last without thought. Maybe because he knew she wouldn't be in until late in the afternoon, or maybe it was because he could slide her comics in a bag and think about the look on her face when she sat on her couch to read them that night. Or maybe she read in bed. Since he hadn't seen her bedroom, he couldn't picture that, but what he could imagine clearly was the spark in her eyes when she opened her issue of *Batgirl*.

She had an unnatural love of bats.

When the last comic was tucked in her bag and all the boxes tossed out back, Adam finally sank onto the stool by the register. He didn't even have enough energy to open a book to read. His phone buzzed in his pocket. A text from Reese:

Got out of class early. On my way. Want a coffee?

I would worship at your feet for the strongest caffeinated thing you can get me.

If I'd known that caffeine was such a huge bargaining chip, I would've used my connections earlier. Be there soon.

His brain was so sleep-deprived that he had no idea how long he sat in a zombie-like state waiting for Reese. She barreled through the door like she always did, bringing a blast of cold air with her. Watching Reese move was always interesting. Head down, long strides, moving quickly like a woman on a mission. But while in the store, she was the opposite. She meandered down the aisle and browsed through things she wouldn't actually read.

As soon as she was mid-store, she looked up and a smile blasted across her face. Then she held up a gigantic cup of coffee. He could kiss her. The thought brought unwanted images to his mind. It was an expression. He didn't need to think about acting on that. It was the lack of sleep and the promise of good caffeine tossing him off balance.

She handed him the cup. "You look like crap."

He took a long drink before responding. "I've

been working a lot. I have the sketches done."

"Already? I thought we were meeting Friday."

"We can. If this looks good, we can move on to the next book. You said we have a tight timeline." Another drink. It was smooth and rich and about as perfect as a cup of coffee could be. "What is in this stuff?"

"A special mixture. I'm thinking of calling it the Goddess Blend. That way I can have men falling at my feet all day." She tapped her gloved hands on the glass counter. "Well? Let's see them."

Right. He was supposed to show her the finished artwork. He tilted his head toward his desk. "I inked and colored the first page. I couldn't help myself. I really wanted to see it in color. But I used a copy, so no worries."

She ran ahead of him, taking off her gloves in the process. Sitting on his stool, she studied the pages. By the third page, her eyes were teary.

Damn. He thought he'd nailed it this time. Reese set the pages on the desk and jumped up. She threw her arms around his neck and hugged him. "Thank you. It's perfect."

Huh? This woman did nothing but confuse him. He stood, not reciprocating the hug and unsure of what to do with his hands. "You like it?"

She stepped back, obviously feeling his awkwardness. "It's exactly what I imagined and couldn't describe. The way you show Alexis's fear, the noise in the background, the subtle changes on the first page that you did in color. It's amazing. I knew you were the right guy for the job." Her eyes had cleared and she smiled at him. "Did you think I'd hate it?"

"You did look upset."

She smacked his arm. "You dummy. I'm a girl. Sometimes I get emotional." Then she rolled her eyes before sitting back on the stool.

Adam went back to the counter to drink his coffee while she looked at the pages. "When do I get the rest of the stories? If this was the shortest, like you were thinking, I need to plan for how many hours of work I'll need."

"You have the next one. I just need to revise it based on having her origin done. You know, fewer flashbacks and stuff. I'll have more time to explore the subplot for that book as well as engage the overarching plot." She glanced over her shoulder at him. "I could probably introduce the mentor in the next issue."

Nothing like a little prompting to go with his afternoon coffee.

She set the pages back on the desk and hopped off the stool. "Come on, Cap'n. You know your guy is perfect as Lyrid's mentor."

"I'll consider it if you promise to stop calling me that."

She took off her jacket and laid it on the stool, the sleeves dragging on the floor. He picked it up and hung it on a hook on the storeroom door.

"What, no witty response?"

"I like my nickname for you. I can pretend it refers to Captain America."

He crossed his arms. "That's a bullshit play on words. We both know you'll be thinking about Captain Atom and that's…awful. People don't even like him. Other superheroes don't trust him."

"Only in the latest versions. He's a military guy

and you have that look to you. All stiff and quiet. And serious. All. The. Time."

"I am not serious all the time."

She waved him off. "Deal. If it bothers you that much, I won't use the name anymore."

Damn. He hadn't counted on her agreeing. She enjoyed making him crazy too much. Did he just sign away his latest creation?

Reese extended her hand. "Your hero is now a mentor."

He took her hand because he didn't know how not to. In his gut, he knew Lyrid needed a mentor, someone to guide her. His gaze locked on Reese's light blue eyes. A strange tension filled the space between them.

Her hand lingered in his a little longer than was polite. Or maybe that was his grasp being late to let go.

Adam slid his palm from hers. "He needs a name. We can't keep calling him my guy. That'll start to take on a whole new connotation."

"Let's start building the rest of his backstory, get him a job, fill in the spaces. A name will come to us." She gathered the pages and restacked them neatly. Her fingertips traced over the top image of Alexis.

That moment filled him with the confidence that he'd chosen the right career for himself. He belonged doing this. He wanted to reach readers the way the greats had reached him: through story and art.

He stared at Reese while she stared at his art.

"Hey, I'm back," his mom called from the door.

Both he and Reese turned to her voice, like

being startled from a dream. If his face looked anything like Reese's, his mom would think they'd been making out on the counter, except they'd been across the room from each other.

"What's going on here?" she asked.

"Hi, Bonnie. It's been a while."

"Bonnie? You know my mom?"

Reese slid from the stool. This was the moment of truth. Would she have a reaction like her mother did? Would she comment on his mom being white, while he clearly was not?

"Well, I didn't know she was your mom, but I know her. I have been in here before, you know. Did you think I only came in to see your ugly mug?"

His mom laughed and tugged off her coat.

Reese spun back to face him. "You totally have her smile. I should've seen it before."

Mom walked by to hang up her coat, still chuckling.

Adam stood with his mouth hanging open. Not only did Reese not have a reaction to his mom, but she didn't even offer up the usual in-correct assumption: *I didn't know you were adopted.* It was like the thought never entered her mind.

"Oh boy, Bonnie. I think I might've really hurt his feelings. He's quieter than usual." Reese waved a hand in front of his face. "Hello…"

He swatted at her flailing palm. "Please. I was busy thinking. We don't have time to compare smiles."

His mom came over and kissed his cheek. "What are you two doing?"

"Reese asked me to work on a comic book with her for her senior project."

"Let me see."

Reese blurted out, "Sure" at the same time he said, "No."

He stepped in front of Reese to block her progress. "It's not finished. It's not ready to show to anyone."

Reese bumped her shoulder into his. "She's your *mom*. Of course she'll say wonderful things, even if it was crap. Which it's not."

His mom chuckled again. He didn't see what the hell was so funny.

Reese handed his mom the pages and he swallowed the last gulps of his coffee before tossing the cup into the can behind the counter. He busied himself with getting Reese's comics for the week. Anything to avoid watching the two women dissect his work.

"Oh, baby. These are fabulous. I wish you'd let me see more of your work." She huddled close to Reese. "He never wants me to see anything. Every time he's working in here, he covers it all up before I can peek."

Reese shook her head at him.

"You're one to talk. You handed me the first story and expressly said I couldn't show it to anyone else."

"That was different." She tilted her head and crossed her arms.

"Not really."

His mom handed the sheets back to Reese. "I can close up tonight if you have some place you'd like to be." Mom's eyebrows shot up. Subtlety was not her strong suit.

"We're just talking."

"Go talk somewhere else. Get some dinner. Go see a movie. Have fun."

"Talking about comics is fun."

She looked to Reese for help in her argument, but Reese shrugged. "He's got you there. We both really like comics."

"Oh, the two of you. To be twenty-two again. I'd show you what life is supposed to be like at your age."

Adam covered his ears. "I don't want to hear what you think we should be doing."

Reese doubled over in laughter as his mom smacked his arms and poked at his abdomen.

"Get out of here. Go have fun. Or work. Or *whatever*. I'll see you tomorrow."

Adam smiled again. One word his mother hated was *whatever*, so the emphasis she placed on it was kind of priceless. He gave up. He wouldn't force Reese to hang out with him. He could just as easily go home and crawl into bed. He handed Reese her jacket and her bag of comics.

When they got outside he said, "Sorry about that. My mom can be pushy."

"I like your mom. She's funny."

"Anyway, you don't have to hang out with me. Your night is free to do whatever." He tucked his hands in his jacket pocket, wishing he had gloves.

"I don't have anything going on. You want to grab dinner?"

"Sure. You pick a place. I'll follow in my car." Friends traveled in separate vehicles. He didn't want to give his mom any more ideas about Reese. Uncomplicated. It was a good way to live.

He followed Reese to some hole-in-the-wall diner. She parked and waited on the sidewalk for him. Pointing at the restaurant behind her, she said, "It doesn't look like much, but they have the best cheese everything here: cheese fries, grilled cheese, mac 'n' cheese, you name it."

"Lead the way. Who doesn't like cheese?" Christ, he sounded dumb.

Inside, they sat in a booth and Reese wiggled out of her coat and squished it in the corner with her bag. A waitress stopped by and set down menus.

Reese slapped her hand on them. "I got this." She looked up at the waitress. "One order of cheese fries." To him, she said, "It's a huge order. We'll split it. Burger?"

He threw up his hands. "Sure."

"Two burgers, two Cokes." Once the waitress left, Reese stared at him.

"What?"

"If I can't call you Captain anymore, you're gonna need a new name."

"I have a name. Adam's good."

"But Cap'n just has a nice ring to it."

He shook his head. "Let's talk about the comic instead. Give your characters all the nicknames you want."

She laughed. He liked the sound.

They talked about story ideas and the waitress came with their food. Reese was right—the cheese fries were the best he'd ever had. The burger, not so much. But hanging out with Reese was worth it.

When they were finished, Adam stood. "I'll go pay the bill."

"You don't have to buy me dinner."

"It's fine."

"I'll leave the tip."

He nodded and walked toward the register as she dug through her bag. While he waited to be rung out, the conversation of the women at the table across from the counter carried to him.

"Like she couldn't get a man of her own, so she had to poach one of ours?"

Adam spun and looked at the woman speaking. She was glaring at Reese.

"How was everything tonight?" the manager asked from behind the register.

He glanced at Reese to see if she'd heard the woman before turning to the manager. "It was great. Thanks." He got his change and hurried back to Reese. He maneuvered her down the other aisle toward the door. He didn't want to invite any further comments.

One sentence ruined his evening. At least Reese hadn't heard. How much worse would it have been if he and Reese had been holding hands or kissing?

For a moment, the questions in his head were replaced by memories of his childhood. Walking with his parents, he heard the remarks. He'd been too young to understand their meaning, but he knew they were hurtful.

His stomach knotted. He couldn't live constantly waiting for the nastiness to come out of people. That was why he needed uncomplicated. Being Reese's friend was enough.

CHAPTER SIX

For the next week, Reese and Adam spoke daily, shooting texts and e-mails back and forth, almost always followed closely by a phone call to argue their points. It was a strange game they played and she enjoyed it. The first book was complete, with ink and color, and she'd be handing it off to her friend Julie today for a final proofread and layout for printing. Julie was the business end of the operation. Her job was production, getting everything organized and to the printer and keeping them on track.

When this whole project was finished, Reese was going to throw one hell of a party to celebrate. She'd asked Julie to pick up the book so she could introduce Julie to Adam. Up until now, Julie hadn't had a role to play and Reese had been the go-between, but with as much as Adam had invested in her project, and in turn, her grade, he should probably get to meet the rest of the team.

She was glad that Adam suggested they work at the shop this afternoon. Their weekend meetings were testing the limits of her control over her crush. They always sat close. How could they not? They hunched over the same pages and discussed character and story and how to portray them. It wasn't something that could be done on opposite ends of a couch.

She knew this because she'd tried. He didn't react to any of her flirtation, os she figured he wasn't interested. She wasn't his type. At least she got a pretty good friend out of the deal. And an awesome artist to work with.

When she got to Comic Universe, Adam was deep in conversation with a couple of guys about a series she knew nothing about. She waved with the cup of coffee she'd brought him as she walked behind the customers and took a seat at his desk. She'd spent so much time here that it was starting to feel more like a home away from home.

Adam walked behind the register and rang the guys out. They left saying they'd see him next week.

"You didn't have to cut it short. I would've waited."

"But then my coffee would be cold." He picked up the cup at her elbow. "What's the bribe for?"

"It's not a bribe. I know you like it and I worked the early shift." She checked her watch. "Julie should be here soon. I can't wait for you to meet her."

"I still don't see why we need another person. We're handling it all okay."

"Publishing companies have entire teams dedicated to what we're doing. I can't do it all. I'm actually amazed that you're doing all of the artwork.

I would've been happy if you got me to the ink phase and I just had to hire someone to color."

The look on Adam's face was priceless, like she'd just lobbed the biggest insult ever.

"What? Everyone has a specialty. I knew you could draw. How was I supposed to know if you could color?" She shifted on the stool and her jacket slid out from under her butt.

Adam bent over and tugged the jacket the rest of the way off the stool and hung it up. "So did you have someone else lined up?"

She spun on the stool to watch him move. "I had someone in mind, but I never talked to him about it. There was nothing to say until I had actual pictures. And then you kept going."

In truth, she was ecstatic that Adam was handling all of the stages of artwork. The only other artist she was familiar with was her ex-boyfriend, Frankie. Although she still saw Frankie every week at their regular RPG night, she really didn't want him to have a piece of her book.

"Promise me that no one else will touch this." Adam's tone was more serious than usual, which she didn't even think possible.

"Julie's it. If she finds a problem, she'll bounce it back to us. With her handling the production end, I can focus on marketing and promotion." She spun back toward the desk, taking in the length of the store as she did. She jumped off the stool. "Oh my God. This is perfect."

"What is?" Adam leaned casually against the counter by the register.

"Would your mom mind if we filmed the campaign ad here?"

"Huh?"

"In order to set up my crowd source campaign to fund the printing of the comic, I need to have a video. Like a commercial. This would be the perfect location."

Adam shrugged. "I don't see why she'd care, but I'll ask."

The door opened and Julie walked in. Reese stared at her a minute. She was decked out in a long red cashmere coat that her boyfriend had bought her. Her blond hair was swept up in a way that Reese couldn't imagine how to do and her cheeks were pink from the cold. She looked slightly older than Reese, especially since Reese still dressed the same way she had since high school.

Not Julie. Julie always looked like she was on her way to a job interview.

"Hi," she said as she walked through the store, pulling her gloves off. "Cute store."

Reese stepped forward. "Julie, this is Adam, our artist. This is his mom's shop. Adam, Julie."

Reese turned and looked at Adam, who smiled at Julie before taking her hand. She didn't miss the appreciative sweep of his gaze over Julie's body. A twinge of jealousy poked her chest. Hadn't she just convinced herself that Adam was good to have as a friend? So what if he was attracted to Julie?

At least she understood why. Reese just wasn't his type. She turned away and grabbed the pages off the desk. "Here it is."

She held the stack out to Julie, who accepted it, but instead of putting it away in her bag, she laid it out on the counter. "This is really good work, guys. Not that I'm an expert in comics or anything."

"What are you an expert in?" Adam asked.

Julie turned her brilliant smile on Adam. "While I love English, I knew there wouldn't be enough money in it for me, so I turned to computers. I'm your publisher."

Adam nodded, but he didn't look convinced that Julie knew what she was talking about.

"Reese, I know you're doing the marketing end, but I think you need to have a few of these panels for advertising. Like blown up bigger." She turned to Adam. "Do you have a problem with that?"

"Making copies of those?"

"Not all of them, but a few key pieces to highlight your work. I'll choose a few to get started and let you see. Then you'll have them for marketing and promotion." She stacked the pages she'd spread out and opened the flap on her light brown leather briefcase to slide them in.

Anxiety tumbled through Reese's stomach. That was their only finished copy. Watching someone else handle it, take it away, made her edgy. She released a slow breath. She trusted Julie and knew Julie would get it right, just like Adam had. They were going to be a success.

"Nice to meet you, Adam. I'm sure we'll be seeing more of each other once things get moving along." Julie pulled her gloves back on. "Want to grab a drink later?" she asked Reese.

"It's Thursday."

"Right. Geek night. I forgot. Give me a call this weekend and we'll chat." As she turned toward the door, she winked at Reese and mouthed, "He's cute."

Yeah, Reese already knew that. Too bad he didn't feel the same.

After Julie left, Adam asked, "Geek night?"

Reese's cheeks flamed. "Uh, yeah. That's what she calls it. I meet with friends on Thursday nights."

"I thought you always worked on Thursdays and that's why you couldn't meet about the comics. So what are you doing?" He sipped his coffee.

Reese bit down hard on her lip. She should be able to tell Adam. Of all the people she knew, he should understand. "We meet weekly to play a tabletop RPG."

"So you're a D&D girl." She heard the smug smile in his voice.

"We don't play Dungeons and Dragons. We play Hero's Crusade."

"Never heard of it."

"It's the same kind of game as D&D. We meet, we go on missions, we battle." She reached for her bag and pulled out her notebook.

For the next two hours, they worked on story, occasionally being interrupted by customers looking for their favorite comics. Some stopped and listened to Adam and Reese discussing plot and characterization before asking for help. Others actually offered input. Useless input, but at least they were showing interest.

Reese glanced at the clock. "I need to get going."

Adam looked at her and asked, "Game time?"

"Yeah." She shoved her notebook into her bag. "If you're not doing anything tonight, you could join us."

As soon the words left her mouth, she regretted them. She shouldn't assume he'd want to hang out with her more than what they needed to do for the book. Plus, her friends hated when outsiders showed up.

He seemed to weigh her invitation, which meant that she couldn't rescind. The best she could hope for was that he wouldn't want to.

"My mom will be here in a little bit to relieve me. Can you wait? I'll follow in my car."

Damn. How was she going to explain him to the guys? "Sure," she answered with a tight-lipped smile.

As soon as he accepted Reese's offer, Adam questioned it. Her face froze and he thought that maybe she didn't really want him to come. Then why invite him? He didn't even know why he'd accepted, other than he wanted to see a different side of Reese. They'd spent a bunch of time together, but he only got to know one side of her: the writer.

He knew the writer pretty well. She was controlling and demanding, yet scattered in her thought process. She was messy. It was the best way to describe her. He wanted to know if she was like that in every aspect of her life.

Before Reese had the chance to say or do anything else, his mom breezed through the door.

Since he didn't have classes on Thursdays, he'd started opening the store so she could have time off. She insisted that she close on those days, though. It was like she couldn't be happy leaving the shop alone for an entire day.

"Hey, Mom."

"Hi, honey. Reese, it's good to see you again. If you become any more of a fixture around here, I'll have to put you to work."

The offhand comment sparked something in Adam's mind. Reese would be good here. She'd already proven it. She hadn't mentioned anything about moving away from Chicago after graduating, so she might be a good fit to replace him. His mom would be in good hands and he would worry less.

Huh. It was a weird feeling to acknowledge that he would trust Reese with his mother. Well, at least the shop.

"You ready?" Reese asked.

"Yeah. See you tomorrow, Mom." He grabbed his jacket and followed Reese out the door.

They drove down to the Lincoln Park area. They were near DePaul University and traffic was thick. Reese pulled into a small parking lot, but didn't park. He pulled up alongside her.

She rolled down her window and said, "You can park here. They only have two guest spots. I know the neighborhood, so I'll find something on the street."

"No. That's crazy. I'll find metered parking." Now he felt bad that not only was he intruding on her night with friends, but she'd lose out on free parking too.

"No." She shook her head and waved. "Hold on. Let me call Lee and see if there's another spot."

She tapped away on her phone while they sat in their cars blocking the path for anyone else who might go by. "Awesome!" She yelled, "Take this spot. Lee has an assigned spot that he's not using because his car's in the shop."

"You sure?"

"Yeah." She rolled up her window and drove away, not giving him a chance to argue.

He pulled in and waited to see where she'd come from. A moment later, she was walking toward him carrying groceries in addition to her usual bag. He got out of the car and met her. He pointed to the tote. "Should I have brought something?"

"Nah. This is just some chips and salsa. The guys will have pop. We take turns bringing food."

She led the way to a three-story walk-up. The building was old, and it didn't look like much had been updated, unlike many of the other buildings around them. Reese shoved through the exterior door and rang a bell. The buzzer sounded and she opened the interior door.

Adam continued to follow her up the stairs. When they got to the third floor, a door on their right opened, but no one greeted them. They took off their coats and hung them on an already over-burdened coatrack.

He looked around the apartment. It was nothing special. A futon sat in the corner with a table smashed against it. They obviously had re-arranged furniture to accommodate the table that three guys were sitting around.

"Hey, everyone. This is Adam." She pointed her thumb over her shoulder at him. She put chips and salsa on the kitchen counter.

Adam stepped forward.

Reese pointed to one guy. "This is Lee. It's his apartment." Adam nodded at him. She moved to the guy on his left. "This is Chris. Where's Kim?"

Chris toyed with the dice in front of him. "She had a final to study for."

Reese looked at Adam over her shoulder. "Kim is the only other girl who plays. Now I'm outnumbered." She turned to the last guy, who was setting up a folder in front of himself. "This is Frankie."

"Are you playing?" Frankie asked.

Nothing like being friendly. "I'm not sure. I just came to hang out with Reese."

"He can play an NPC for the night. That's okay, right, Frankie?"

Adam nudged her shoulder. "NPC?"

"Non-player character. It's a character that he can create for just tonight's mission."

"He doesn't even know what he's doing, Reese. Who the hell did you bring?"

Reese reached behind her and tugged on Adam's sleeve. "He's a friend who wanted to check out the game." She pushed Adam toward the seat beside Chris and she sat between Adam and Frankie.

"Stop being a dick," Lee said.

"Whatever." Frankie set some papers behind his screen.

Adam leaned over and whispered, "I'm really okay just watching. I don't want to mess up your game."

"There's nothing to mess up. It's like a story that unfolds as we play. You'll catch on." She pulled a small pouch from her bag. "You can use my dice. We'll explain as we go."

Frankie was scribbling away behind his cardboard screen. Reese, Lee, and Chris all started talking about where they had left off last week, and Reese kept breaking off to offer Adam insight and explanation. It all sounded very complicated. The more he listened, the more he believed this had been a colossal mistake.

And then they started to play.

Frankie looked at him and said, "You can be a dwarf who is searching for the magic potion to save his village."

"A dwarf?"

"Yeah."

Reese snickered.

"What are you?" he asked her.

"An elfin archer."

He could see her as an elf. Not much better than a dwarf. He looked at Lee.

"I'm a knight."

Chris said, "I'm a sorcerer."

"Why can't I be a knight?"

"Because you're just playing today. Knights play important ongoing roles," Frankie answered. "Let's start."

As Frankie explained the mission for the night, Adam focused on what he needed to do. It seemed simple enough. Roll the dice to determine what happened. He could follow this.

Frankie continued, "You enter the cave and discover no light source. What do you do?"

Reese's eyebrows nearly joined. "How big is the mouth to this cave?"

Frankie shrugged. "Six."

"What does it smell like?"

Frankie narrowed his eyes. "Bat shit."

Reese opened her mouth to argue, but Chris spoke quickly, as if he knew the question-and-answer session would keep going. "I'll cast a spell to create an orb of light."

"Your light has just awakened the ogre. Prepare to battle."

Reese, Lee, and Chris argued over a battle plan.

Adam spoke up. "How about you guys distract him and I'll sneak around him. Ogres are huge, right? And I'm a little guy."

All three of them stared at him like he was nuts. But Frankie spoke. "No, I called for a battle. They can't pretend."

"Okay. You guys battle and I'll wiggle my little ass by to collect the precious stones we need from the other end of the cave."

Lee said, "I draw my broad sword."

Reese added, "I have my arrows ready."

They each rolled their dice and then Reese slid hers over to Adam again. He rolled a five.

Frankie laughed. "You just fell into a pit."

"But we defeated the ogre," Reese said.

"He didn't complete his part of the mission," Frankie said, pointing at Adam.

Adam asked, "How deep is the pit?"

"Eight feet."

Frankie wanted him out of the picture. Adam knew there was something going on there. Lee and Chris didn't seem bothered by his presence, but Frankie was a different story.

"So we rescue him," Reese said. She winked at Lee. Seriously, a flirtatious wink. "Lower me down, would you?"

Frankie wanted to argue with the unorthodox plan. It was like he had a picture of how things were supposed to go and if someone deviated from his concept, he got pissed off.

It took three tries, but they rescued him. The game went on, and over the next couple of hours, Frankie had tried to kill Adam no fewer than four times. He'd only completed his mission to find the potion because Reese had been looking out for him.

Adam waited by the door as Reese said her good-byes so he could walk out with her. Over the course of the night, he'd seen another side to her, but what he found interesting was that she was the writer everywhere. Even here, her purpose was to build story. She had fun and got caught up in the details, details that had been lacking in the first written story she'd given him.

She gave Lee a huge hug and whispered something to him. Adam felt like a voyeur, but at the same time, he wanted to be close enough to eavesdrop. What did she have to say to Lee that she couldn't say loud enough for everyone to hear? She hugged Chris too, but it was shorter, and when she pulled away, she told him to wish Kim good luck on her final. When she turned to Frankie, she just nodded and said good-bye.

Adam held her coat out for her to slide into. "All set?"

"Yep."

They walked in silence down the flights of stairs. At the bottom, before going out into the cold, she said, "I should apologize."

"For what?"

"Frankie." She heaved out a sigh. "I really thought it'd be okay by now. He's my ex-boyfriend."

That explained a whole lot about how his night had gone.

Reese pulled her gloves on. "It's been a long time, and we've continued to play the game every week. I've known these guys for years, and I didn't want to leave the group because of my failed relationship with him."

"I'm guessing you've never brought another guy to the game, though."

"No. And I should've thought of that. I figured we'd be okay since you and I aren't… I mean, we're friends. It's not like I'd ask my new boyfriend to hang out with my ex. But Frankie's Frankie."

"I had fun anyway." He held the exterior door open for her.

"You did?"

"Yeah." As odd as it seemed. "I didn't think I would, but watching you create a story on the fly like that was pretty amazing."

Her cheeks were pink and he didn't know if it was the cold or if she was blushing, but it was cute.

"Can I ask you something?"

"Shoot," she said.

"Lyrid's origin, well, Alexis's story. How much of that is autobiographical?"

They'd walked past his car and were nearly at hers. She bit her lip, but when her eyes met his, they were clear and sure.

"If you want to talk, get in the car. It takes forever for this beast to warm up." She unlocked the doors and climbed in. He got in on the other side and waited.

She started the engine and stared out the windshield at the brick building in front of them. "How'd you know?"

"There was a lot of emotion when Alexis heard her parents fighting. The fear she felt came across the page too realistically."

"Maybe I'm just that good of a writer."

He chuckled. "I wasn't implying that you're not. It was a lucky guess then."

"My dad beat my mom. I used to hear them fighting. He always had certain expectations for the house, my mom, me. If something wasn't just right, she paid the price. So that part was real. Being struck by a meteorite and having the power to kill my dad? Not so much. When I was ten, my mom left him and took me with her. I haven't seen him since."

Adam was speechless. Although he'd suspected, he hadn't really thought about what having this conversation would be like. He went with his gut. "That's shitty."

She turned to look at him with a slight smile on her face. "Yeah, it was."

He reached out and brushed her hair back over her shoulder away from her face. He needed to touch her, make sure she was okay now. Her smile widened, but her eyes were still sad. The air around them charged with tension.

Something in her car made a loud rattling noise. He stared at the dash like it might explode.

"Don't worry. That's just the heater letting me know it's okay to drive now."

"Thanks for telling me about your dad."

"Thanks for asking."

As if that took effort. Pulling away from her now, though, did take effort. He popped the door open and stepped out. "See you this weekend? We can work at my apartment if you want. My roommate will be working late."

"Sure. See you then."

He closed the door and jogged back to his car, unsure of what he was thinking. Hanging out with her friends, making her ex jealous and getting off on it, and asking personal details was not a way to steer clear of complicated relationships. But something about Reese kept drawing him in. He just didn't know what to do about it.

CHAPTER SEVEN

Reese had spent the last few days working furiously on rewriting her first comic so that she and Adam would have something to work on Saturday night. She'd been uneasy since their last conversation in her car. While she didn't keep it a secret, she rarely talked about her dad.

Knowing that Adam had figured it out based on the comic should've made her feel better. It meant that she'd done something right with the story. However, there was always the fear that Adam would look at her differently now. They'd become friends and she didn't want to strain that.

Of course, inviting him to hang out with her ex-boyfriend hadn't been the smartest move. Frankie had been an asshole all night. Maybe it was time for her to move on and find a new group to play with, but she really hated the idea of walking away from Lee, Chris, and Kim. They'd become her friends as much as they were Frankie's. That was probably the worst part of a breakup—deciding who got the friends. And with

Frankie, so much of their lives had been inter-twined: school, work, play.

Finishing the anthology and publishing it would be a definite sign of moving on. It was something that was completely separate from any-thing she'd done with Frankie. Adam's ability to handle all the artwork made it that much sweeter.

She listened to her phone give her directions to Adam's house. As she drove through the residen-tial neighborhood, she immediately felt out of place. This was the kind of neighborhood she'd dreamed of living in when she was younger. After a string of crappy one-bedroom apartments with her mom, anything started to look good, but this neighborhood held a mix of single-family homes and two- and three-flat apartments. A light dusting of snow that had fallen earlier that day coated the lawns, making everything more pic-turesque.

This was a different kind of jealousy than she had when she went to visit Lee. His apartment was young, urban professional. It was about being part of city life, walking to the store and easy access to the beach. Adam's neighborhood was more fam-ily-oriented, as evidenced by the number of mini-vans lining the street. She could imagine the trees being full of leaves in the summer, providing shade as kids ran through sprinklers.

She then wondered why Adam and his friend chose to live here. He'd said his friend was a musi-cian. It seemed like an odd choice. She found some parking down the block from the two-flat that Adam lived in. She raced up the sidewalk because the wind had picked up and slashed against her cheeks. Stomping her feet for warmth, she rang the bell. Adam met her at the door.

He held out a little piece of paper. "You need to put this on your dash. Permit parking."

She groaned. "Here." She handed him her bag. "I'll be right back." She jogged back down the block and put the permit in the window and ran back. By the time she got inside, her lungs were burning both from being out of breath and from the cold.

"Sorry. I just remembered about the permit."

"Permit parking is stupid."

"Yeah, well, that's the city. Come on in and warm up." He led the way into the first-floor apartment.

The door opened into a huge living room–dining room combination. What should've been the living room looked more like a music studio, with instruments lined up everywhere, along with amps and speakers. The dining room space was being used as the living room with a single comfy-looking couch and TV unit. They had milk crates for a coffee table.

"Where are we going to work?"

"I have drafting tables in my bedroom." He stopped midstride, as if realizing what he'd just said. "Unless that makes you uncomfortable. Then we can work in here on the floor."

"I'm fine wherever. I think I can trust you to behave yourself. Or have you been secretly doing all of this work on my comic as a ploy to get me to your bedroom all along? Maybe it's not even a bedroom, but a dungeon and you plan to chain me up."

He laughed, but it was an uncomfortable, you-sound-crazy kind of laugh. He shoved a door open. "Totally normal bedroom."

She sighed. "I'm a little disappointed."

"You're weird."

She couldn't stop the smile. "I know. And you like me anyway."

"Yeah, I do."

She stepped into his bedroom and he hadn't lied. His bed was pushed into a corner to make room for two drafting tables on the opposite wall. A cheap nightstand stood beside the bed. A small bookcase was wedged behind the door, but that was it for furniture.

Reese dropped her bag beside one of the tables.

"Oh, shit. Hang on." Adam left the room and returned with a chair. "It was either this or the little stool Hunter uses for his drums."

"That's fine." It was a battered, old dining room chair and looked far from comfortable, but she could always sit on his bed and talk. He needed the desk more than she did.

Adam sat on his stool, one that sat on rollers and spun in circles, but didn't appear much more comfortable than the chair she had. She pulled her notebook out. "I reworked the story for the first book featuring Lyrid. I wrote in the mentor. It's up to you to decide if I got it right."

She flipped to the page and handed him the book. Again, she found herself waiting while he read. She should have sent him the story ahead of time to be more efficient. Waiting was painful.

Luckily, Adam was a fast reader. He set the notebook on the desk and spun to face her. "It's missing something. There's not enough action. You've introduced the mentor, who still doesn't have a name, but all he does is watch. He's not a mentor yet. We don't know who he is, and that's all right, but other than Alexis freaking out and doing her mind-control stuff, nothing happens."

"Stuff happens." She grabbed the book and scanned for examples. While she reread her work, she tried to imagine it on the page, what each panel would show. Two pages in, she knew she'd messed up. "Damn. How did I screw that up so badly?"

"It's not screwed up. You just cut so much from the earlier draft, the flashbacks, that you lost all action. It's like this is a continuation of her origin story. We don't need that now. What if we just skip to the part where she decides to use her powers for good? Or at least decides to use them at all?"

Even as he spoke, new ideas entered Reese's mind. She saw plot points as pictures. Excitement sparked just like it had when they'd first discussed her writing an origin story for Lyrid. She grabbed her notebook and began to scribble description and dialogue for each panel. As soon as she had a panel written, she ripped the page from the notebook and handed it to Adam to start sketching.

For an hour they worked seamlessly, barely saying more than a few words to each other. They'd reached the climax of the story, where Alexis would meet her mentor. Gunner. That would be his name.

She set the notebook back down and waited for Adam to sketch, but he moved too slowly.

Snaking her right hand around his left as his pencil shaded something, she created a text box and wrote, "Gunner watches Alexis from the shadows."

The sensitive skin on the inside of her arm skimmed along Adam's. His warmth spread across her and she focused on the letters in front of her.

"What are you doing?"

Reese tilted her head and looked at him from under her lashes before going back to her lettering. "You're taking too long. He has a name."

Adam's hand stopped moving on the page, and she missed the friction against her own skin. They sat shoulder to shoulder and she felt Adam's eyes on her.

"In my defense, sketching people takes longer than writing a few words."

"I know. I'm impatient."

Adam flipped his pencil deeper between his fingers and used his tips to push her hand away. "Gunner, huh?"

"It's perfect."

"Why does he only watch from the shadows?" Adam asked.

His breath whispered across her cheek. Her voice lowered as she spoke. "Because he knows her. He sees her even though she tries to remain invisible."

"When does he come out of the shadows?"

Reese tilted her head slightly and her eyes rose to meet Adam's. "When he sees she needs him. He likes the shadows. He likes to watch, to keep his distance."

"Until he can't."

Her heart thumped in her chest. The dark gray of Adam's eyes was nearly swallowed by his pupils. Oxygen leaked into her lungs. She nodded in understanding—both for the words he said and the action she hoped he'd take.

His movement was infinitesimal as his gaze swept over her face and landed on her lips. Her eyelids fluttered. She wanted this so badly.

Adam said nothing as he closed the remaining distance between their mouths. His full lips caressed hers before opening and interlocking with hers. She sighed with relief and enjoyment. He shifted and tilted to change the angle, but made no other movement to touch her.

She surged forward, dropping her pencil and turning her body to fully face him. Opening her lips, she swiped her tongue against his. Oh man, did he feel good.

A *thunk* at the other end of the house registered in her head, but she didn't move.

"Yo, Adam. I need help."

At the sound of his name, Adam shot back away from her, his stool sliding across the floor. His chest rose and fell in the same fast succession as hers.

"I…uh…sorry. I don't know what that was."

Reese smirked, but before she could respond, Adam's friend was standing in the doorway.

"Oh, hey. I have the booze for the party. I need help carrying it in."

"I thought you were working tonight."

He shrugged. "They canceled the second set. The place was empty. No one wants to go out in the cold." He stepped forward. "Hi, I'm Hunter."

Reese extended a hand. "Reese."

"I've seen you before. The comic shop, right?"

"Yeah." She stood. "I can help you carry stuff in."

Adam rushed past her. "We got it."

"Don't listen to him. I'm double-parked and we can use help."

ADAM RAN OUT THE FRONT DOOR WITHOUT HIS coat and hoped the frigid air would cool his entire system. He had no idea what had come over him. Reese was just so close and she smelled good and the soft skin of her arms brushed against his. Then she spoke in that whispery, husky voice and he about blew a nut right there.

He pulled the hatch open on Hunter's van and leaned in to grab a box. Behind him he heard, "You drive a minivan? Cute."

Crap. Why couldn't she have just waited inside?

"Not cute. Practical. It hauls all of my music equipment," Hunter answered.

Adam hefted a box, glass clinking together inside, and stepped back. "Where'd all this come from?"

"The manager at work got us an excellent deal."

Hunter's smile told Adam he didn't want to know what the deal was. He walked around Hunter and used the box to shield the half boner he still sported. Behind him, Reese laughed. The sound echoed across the empty block and sent a shiver down his spine. She had a great laugh.

He stomped up the stairs and slid the box onto the floor. When he turned, both Hunter and Reese were right behind him. Hunter handed him a box. "I gotta go park. Take care of this."

He accepted the box and Reese followed him into the living room, where they both set their boxes against the wall behind the couch. He exhaled a deep breath. "Hey, about…" He pointed toward the bedroom.

The smile disappeared from her face. She toed the box of alcohol closer to the wall. "Don't worry about it. We were caught up in the moment. A lot of tension as we created great stuff."

His shoulders relaxed. Her reaction was a little too easy, which bugged him, even though it was what he'd wanted. He knew it wasn't right, but he'd thought she wanted the kiss, that it was more than being caught up in the moment.

"So…I was thinking that for the overall relationship between Gunner and Lyrid…" She paused and looked directly into his eyes. "I think they need to hook up."

"No way. That'll never work."

"Why not?"

"A ton of reasons." He ticked them off on his fingers. "He's her mentor. He's older than she is and a felon. He's supposed to protect her." Adam sighed and gave voice to the biggest reason. "You'll alienate readers with an interracial couple."

Reese stiffened and then stepped closer, anger blazing in her eyes. "They belong together because they understand each other in ways no one else can. It's our story. If readers don't like it, they don't have to read it."

Just then, Hunter came back into the apartment with yet another box. "Dude, we are going to be so hammered next week."

He crossed the room and added his box to the stack, oblivious to the tension between Adam and Reese. "I have my flyer designed and ready for copies. You have a date yet?"

Adam swallowed hard. He hadn't given a date any thought.

"Invite the world it is, then." Hunter rubbed his hands together like an evil genius.

"I have a date. Reese is coming." He said it and then hoped Reese would be willing to play along. He stared at her. "Hunter agreed to keep the guest list for our annual New Year's Eve party manageable as long as both Free and I had dates."

Her eyes were wide as she absorbed what he said. He willed her to understand and not blow this. Last year was a disaster.

"And why would you want a party to be manageable?" she asked. Her tone was still a little stiff, and Adam feared where she was going with this.

"That's what I'm saying," Hunter said.

Adam shot him a dirty look. "Because last year, our apartment was filled with a bunch of strangers who wouldn't leave. They puked everywhere, broke our table, and got the cops called."

Her face broke out in a soft smile. "Oh. Well, then, I guess it's good that I'm here to help you hold up your end of the bargain, huh?"

Adam got the impression that he was going to pay dearly for this. He looked at Hunter, who was already opening his saxophone case. "Keep it down tonight, would you? We have work to do."

"Gotcha." He winked at Reese, which annoyed Adam. "See you later."

As they walked back to his bedroom, Reese said, "Your roommate's cute. What's the deal about the date?"

"Hunter always has a date. Always. He believes if we don't have dates for our own party, it makes us losers. Thanks for not giving me away back there. I swear I still smell puke in certain corners of the apartment."

Her nose scrunched up in disgust. "I didn't need to know that."

"Anyway, you don't really have to come to the party. He knows I have a date and that's all that matters." He tucked his hands in his pockets because he really wanted to reach out and pull her close again. He needed to get a handle on this attraction or they'd never get any work done.

"You're in luck because I haven't made any plans yet."

Damn. He didn't think she'd want to come. "Cool. We start around seven, but you can show up whenever." He edged back to his stool to work.

"Don't think we won't be revisiting Gunner and Lyrid's relationship."

He knew he wouldn't get off that easy. As he swiveled into place, Reese scooted her chair a little farther away. She picked up the pages he'd already sketched and began adding text and dialogue. They worked in silence, except for the whiny sound of a blues song that Hunter played on the other side of the apartment. Adam didn't know which was more distracting, having Reese close enough to touch or having her ignore him completely.

He shouldn't have kissed her. It had been a mistake, and he had to keep reminding himself of that. They had a good friendship going, as well as an excellent partnership for work.

Besides, as a couple they would never make it. One look at his parents and he knew that. The thought made him a little sick because it was wrong, as wrong as Reese assuming his race didn't matter. Maybe not to him or her, but to plenty of other people, it did matter. He didn't want the complications that would come from that.

Which made him feel like a total shit.

CHAPTER EIGHT

Reese tormented herself all week. She couldn't reconcile the steamy kiss she'd shared with Adam with his attitude that they shouldn't have done it. For all the times she was sure that he wasn't interested in her, that kiss said different. Now she was faced with going to a New Year's Eve party with him and his friends and a bunch of strangers. Maybe in the relaxed atmosphere of a party, she could get him to open up to figure out what he was thinking.

She looked at her wardrobe, not knowing what to wear to the party. Nothing screamed *kiss me like that again*, so she'd called Julie to ask for help. She had no idea why she continued to stare at her closet like something would change. Jeans, cargo pants, T-shirts, and sweatshirts. She only owned one dress, and that was for funerals. She needed something sexy.

From the other side of the apartment, her mom called, "Julie's here!"

"Come in," Reese yelled.

Julie walked into the bedroom carrying a filled

garment bag. Reese didn't even own a garment bag. Laying the bag on the bed, Julie said, "I brought a bunch of stuff because you didn't say how formal this thing is."

Reese shrugged. "A party at Adam's apartment. Not formal at all, I guess."

"What look are you going for?"

Another shrug.

One of Julie's eyebrows winged up.

"Fine. I want to be sexy. I want him to have to pick his tongue up off the floor. I want him to kiss me like he did last week."

Julie's arms dropped from where they were un-zippering the bag. "He kissed you?"

Reese nodded. "It was so great. Until his roommate interrupted and then Adam apologized, so I let it go." She was still kicking herself for that. She should've kissed him again and turned his world upside down. But he'd seemed so confused by everything that she'd taken pity on him.

"So our mission is to wow his socks off." Julie flipped through some of the clothes on hangers, shaking her head or making faces at each as she moved by.

Reese tried to look over her shoulder to check out the choices, but Julie blocked her view.

"This," she finally said and straightened while tugging a dress from the pile.

Reese stared at it. Calling it a dress was optimistic. It looked like a tube with a complicated maze of straps on the top. "What is that?"

"Trust me." Julie took it off the hanger and held it against Reese. It barely reached mid-thigh.

Given that Julie was a few inches taller, it probably just covered her ass.

How was Reese supposed to walk in this?

"Just try it on."

Julie handed her the dress and waited while Reese stripped down to her bra and panties. Julie pointed at her chest. "No bra. It's built in."

Reese tossed her bra, shimmied into the dress, and tried to figure out how to make the straps look right. Julie tugged and pulled and showed her how it worked. It was freezing in the skimpy dress. Julie dragged her over to the mirror.

The complicated straps wove across her right shoulder, but her left one remained bare. The dress was clingy, but not suffocating. She turned, looking at her whole body, and felt exposed, but she was sexy. "How do you do this every day?"

"Do what?" Julie asked.

"Dress like this. It takes a lot of work and it's not that comfortable." She turned again, liking the way the material showed off her curves.

"I don't dress up every day. I dress for the part I'm playing. I look professional because I want to be taken seriously. When I'm on a date, I want the guy to wonder what's going on underneath my clothes. But when I'm home watching TV and munching on popcorn, I'm all about my yoga pants."

Reese laughed. She couldn't imagine Julie looking anything other than perfect.

"You're going to want fancy shoes, so I brought a few pairs. No combat boots with this dress."

While Reese hadn't really thought about

wearing boots, she cringed at the sight of the heels Julie pulled out of the bag. "I can't wear those."

"Try." She dropped them on the floor near Reese's feet.

Reese stepped into them, and discovered they weren't as painful as she'd thought they'd be. She took a couple of steps and wobbled only once.

"I think you should come with me to the party. Adam's roommate is really cute." She probably shouldn't offer Hunter up since Adam said Hunter always had a date.

"Sorry. I already have plans. With my *boyfriend*. You'll be fine. Besides, if I came, you'd have someone to hang out with. This way, Adam will feel bad leaving you alone since you don't know anyone."

"I don't want a pity date."

"It's not pity. It's using the situation to your advantage." Julie shoved clothes back into the garment bag. "Need anything else?"

"I hope not."

After Julie left, Reese stumbled around in the heels for a while longer to get used to them. When it was time to get ready for the party, she stood in the bathroom and just stared at her makeup. She normally didn't wear much; she was a simple girl. Maybe she should've asked Julie to help with this too.

Her mom walked by the bathroom. "What's wrong?"

"Nothing. I need to get ready for Adam's party and I'm trying to figure out my makeup."

"I saw the dress. Pretty."

Reese nodded and continued to stare at her meager pile of makeup.

Her mom sighed. "Come here." She turned her and pushed her to sit on the closed toilet. "Close your eyes."

Then she started to apply makeup. She hummed while she worked, and Reese relaxed under her mother's care. Taking care of people was her mom's specialty. "So you like this Adam a lot, huh?"

Reese bit back her sigh. "Yeah, but I don't think it's mutual."

"Hmm." Her mom continued to stroke brushes across Reese's face. "Does he treat you right?"

"I just said we're not like that. We're friends and we have fun together, but we're not a couple. As a friend, he treats me fine."

Her mother's hand tilted her chin up, and Reese opened her eyes. "Well, that's a start."

Reese smiled. Her mom had pretty low expectations when it came to men. "Treating you right" could mean any number of things, so the guy could still be a total jerk.

She stood and looked at her reflection above the sink. Her mom had given her smoky eyes and a hint of color on her lips. "Thanks. It looks great. One day, I'll even pay attention so I can do this myself." She brushed a kiss across her mom's cheek and rushed out of the room to get dressed.

She wasn't ready until seven thirty. She didn't want to be the first person at the party, but she didn't want to be so late that she wouldn't be able to find Adam in the crowd. She stared at the present she'd bought for Adam. They hadn't dis-

cussed buying each other gifts, and really, this was
something practical, but she debated bringing it
with her tonight. Ultimately she decided to slide
the package into the pocket of her borrowed coat.
When she got there, she could assess if tonight
was a good idea.

BY THE TIME SHE FOUND A PLACE TO PARK THAT
didn't require a permit, Reese was two blocks
from the party. She eyed her completely imprac-
tical shoes and wished for her boots. At least it
hadn't snowed again, so the sidewalks were mostly
clear. She took a deep breath, tightened the coat
around her, and flung open her door. Damn, it
was cold out.

She hurried down the block, wind whipping at
her. Her toes were instantly numb. Who the hell
dressed like this? It was crazy. When she got to
Adam's apartment, she could hear music through
the door. She rang the bell and when no one answered, she turned the knob. The door opened to
warmth and noise.

Inside the hall she stood for a minute, just ab-
sorbing all the heat she could. Then she proceeded
to Adam's apartment door. Again, she turned the
doorknob and let herself in. She eased through the
door and took in the sight of the crowd. For a
party that had supposedly started only an hour
ago, it was definitely in full swing. She scanned the
partygoers looking for Adam.

Hunter found her first. "Hey, you're here. I
thought maybe Adam was playing me." He

reached for her coat. "I'll put this in Adam's room for you."

Reese thought about it. She was still really cold. "I'll take it. I know the way. Do you know where Adam is?"

Hunter pointed to the corner of the living room. "He's over there doing tattoos."

"Tattoos?"

"Temporary ones. He does them every year. He's really good."

Reese undid the belt of her coat and let it slide open. The warmth of the room hit her. Hunter stared. She blushed under his scrutiny. "What?"

"I want to see the rest." He smiled without being lecherous.

She slid the coat off and hung it over one arm. Then she took a turn. "Anything else?"

Hunter let out a whistle. "You might want to find Adam before anyone else takes notice."

"Sure." She knew she looked good, but she'd never been one to draw attention from every guy in a room. She headed toward Adam's bedroom with her coat, the package of pens banging against her thigh. She debated whether she should take them out now or wait.

Her plan of dumping off her coat in Adam's room was interrupted when she felt someone staring. She looked up and over her shoulder. Her gaze met Adam's.

He held a woman's arm in his hand, marker poised over her skin, but his full attention was on Reese. He mumbled something to the woman in front of him and released her. Then he walked toward Reese, taking no notice of anyone else around him. His staring was a million times worse than Hunter's. She edged away from him and continued on to his room.

Before laying her coat on his stool by his desk, she removed the neatly wrapped package.

From the door, Adam said, "Hey."

"Hi." She turned and held out the box. "Merry Christmas."

"Oh, uh…"

Her hand wavered. "I know we didn't say we were exchanging gifts. I just wanted to get you something small to say thanks for helping with my project."

"I have something for you too. Hold on." He went over to his closet and pulled out a gift bag. "I'm not good at wrapping."

They made the exchange and Reese didn't wait for him to open his present. Inside the bag, she found a couple of notebooks, identical to the ones she preferred to write in, and a Batgirl bobblehead. The sound of paper tearing made her look up. "I hope they're the right kind. I figured by the time you're done with all the coloring for our books, you'd be ready for a new set."

He flipped up the lid on the box of pens. "They're perfect. Thanks."

"This too." She held up the bag, and wanted to say more, but had no idea what.

He stood close, and he continued to let his eyes wander over her, like he'd never seen her before. Of course, he'd never seen her like this, so in a way, she was new.

"I hear you're a tattoo artist, huh?"

He licked his lips, which made her insides flutter.

"Just markers for fun."

"Do one for me?"

"Um, sure. What do you want?"

She turned and set her bag on the floor next to the stool. She stepped closer. "You decide. I trust you."

A slow grin eased across his face. "I know exactly what to do. I've been toying with an idea for Alexis. You can be my practice canvas."

Something about the way he spoke made her knees weak. "Okay," she whispered, knowing no other words would make it out of her mouth.

He spun the stool behind her. "Sit. I'll be right back."

Grateful to give her legs the break they needed to hide their wobbliness, she scooted onto the stool, and tried to keep her dress from sliding inappropriately high. She tugged at the hem as Adam left the room. While he was gone, she took a few slow, deep breaths.

He returned with two markers: one black, one silver. "You sure you trust me?"

"It's only marker, so it'll wash off eventually."

He came closer and his thighs brushed her knees. He reached out and touched the bare skin above the strapless side of her dress. "I'm thinking right here, where Alexis was hit with the power of the meteorite." His fingers trailed up and over her shoulder. "And then it'll continue over here."

His touch was gentle and sensuous. Her heart raced and she struggled to keep her breaths even.

Trying to appear unaffected, she said, "Let's see what you got."

Adam brushed her hair off her shoulder and the cool cap from the marker glided across her skin. Her breath caught. She had no idea what imaginary lines Adam saw, but she knew that look on his face. He was picturing what would be there. A couple of times, the marker ran into the top of her dress. Both times, he huffed in frustration.

Reese smiled. "Here." She reached up and inched the dress down a bit. The top of her boob offered him more canvas.

Without acknowledging the fact that she offered more bare flesh—what was she thinking?—he continued to pretend to draw on her. Then without warning, he stretched alongside her body and hit a lever to lower the stool. The sudden drop caught her by surprise and she squeaked.

"Sorry," he mumbled. "I'm tired of stooping."

Except now she was staring right at the button of his jeans. But then he knelt in front of her, which put his line of sight at her chest.

"Hold still," he said as he uncapped a marker.

She tried to see what he planned to draw, but since he was left-handed, she saw nothing but the back of his hand and some random lines. In an effort to keep her hormones in check, she stared at the ceiling and tried to forget how close Adam stood or how easy it would be to lean forward and steal a kiss.

dam needed to focus. Tuning out the noise from the party was easy enough. Ignoring his senses around Reese was a different story. He had to block almost everything: the silky feel of her skin under his fingertips, the thump of her heartbeat, the soft scent of her perfume, her breath hitching when the cold ink stroked her, the fact that a nipple was a mere inch from his face. He could cause a wardrobe malfunction and have that nipple in his mouth in a second. He clamped his jaw tight.

He closed his eyes momentarily and let the art take over. When he reopened his eyes, Reese was looking up at the ceiling. Not having her stare at him made it easier.

With his concentration intact, his fingers flew over her skin, quickly marking a path. He worried about mistakes and not being able to erase, but once he started, he knew it was right. He'd been thinking about this image for days, sketching it on random pieces of paper, trying to get it perfect.

"Can I see?" Reese asked.

"Not 'til I'm done."

He had no idea how long they sat there in silence while he worked. The black ink on her pale skin mesmerized him. The swell of her gorgeous tit tormented him. He had the main star complete and was working on the stardust pattern over her shoulder when Hunter called from the door, breaking their bubble of solitude.

"Here you are. A bunch of people are looking for you to tattoo them."

Adam's fingers froze on Reese's shoulder. He glared at Hunter. "I'll be done in a minute."

Hunter chuckled. "Maybe close and lock the door next time. Sock on the knob."

"Shut the hell up."

"For real, when are you going to be done? I need your help." Hunter leaned against the doorjamb, but Adam knew that look in his eyes. He was worried about something.

"Two minutes."

Hunter shifted like he didn't believe it.

"Time me."

Sure as shit, Hunter pulled out his phone and tapped away. Adam stood and held the skin taut as he added the finishing touches. He stepped back and looked from a few angles. It was good. He recapped the markers and said, "Okay, you can look now."

Reese glanced down at her chest with wide eyes. She stood and went to his closet to look in the mirror. She turned and studied it much like he had.

"Well?"

"It's amazing. You could do this for a living."

"Nah. I don't like needles."

She gingerly touched the spray of silver and black as if she thought it might rub off. Then she readjusted the top of her dress, covering the swell of flesh he wanted to taste. "Thank you."

"Hey, dude, can I talk to you?"

Hunter still stood in the doorway, waiting. Adam followed him out, reluctant to leave Reese. Over his shoulder, he said, "Drinks and food are in the kitchen. Help yourself, I'll be back in a minute." At least he hoped he would.

Hunter dragged him into the far corner of the living room. "I need your help."

"With what?"

"Amy, Lisa, and Kelly are all here."

"So?"

"I didn't invite them."

"Again, so?"

"I have a date planned for tonight. And it isn't any of them."

Adam couldn't help but laugh. Hunter's social life was finally coming back to bite him in the ass. But then he remembered last year's disastrous fight. "These aren't the same girls from last year, are they?"

Hunter shook his head. "No, but they worry me."

"What am I supposed to do about them?"

"Keep them away from Sydney. And me."

"First of all, who the hell is Sydney?"

"My date. She's our drummer for tonight."

Adam shook his head. "How do you suggest I keep them away?"

"Use your imagination. Tell them what a horrible guy I am. Introduce them to other guys. Tell them to leave. I don't care."

Adam looked into his best friend's eyes. Hunter was really worried about this. "Why not just tell Sydney that these old girlfriends are here? I find that being honest with a girl goes pretty far."

"Because she'll leave. She'll think I'm playing games and leave."

Although he hated asking, he had to. "Are you?"

"Playing games? No."

Then Adam saw the reason for the worry. It wasn't that Hunter thought a fight might break out or he might be embarrassed. He really liked this girl. She mattered. Adam sighed. "I'll try, but if they're all here without an invite, they probably have a reason."

"And I doubt it's good. If you and Free could convince them to leave, I'd owe you."

Adam rolled his eyes. "Do I know these girls?" The names didn't sound familiar, but he rarely paid attention to who Hunter was dating. Mostly because *dating* was a term Hunter used loosely.

Hunter made a few quick, shifty looks around. "Okay, over my left shoulder, red sweater. That's Lisa. Hanging in the doorway to the kitchen in a green dress is Amy."

Adam easily found the two women in question. "And Kelly?"

"I don't see her right now, but she's wearing jeans and a Northwestern sweatshirt." He looked around again. "Sydney should be here soon, so I'm going to go warm up."

"Did you try telling these girls that you have a girlfriend? Maybe they'd take a hint." Adam began to look for Reese. He'd seen her leave the bedroom and go to the kitchen, but not come back.

"I tried. They laughed. Three conversations, three women, and they all thought I was kidding."

"Good luck. I'll see what I can do. Have you talked to Free?"

"Yeah. He's moping around here somewhere looking like a lost Doctor Who. Thanks for your help."

"Sure." Adam looked at the two women in question and since they made no move toward Hunter, he decided to find Reese first. She knew no one at the party and he felt bad leaving her alone.

In the kitchen, he found her surrounded by a group of people, mostly guys who were all admiring her tattoo. He didn't like other people commenting on something that was their private moment. He liked it even less when guys hit on her.

He poured himself a beer from the keg and drank half before interrupting the Reese lovefest. He had no right to be mad or jealous. He'd told her that getting together would be a mistake. He knew it would be a mistake.

"Hey, Reese, can I get you a drink?"

Her face softened when she looked up at him. "A beer would be great. Thanks."

A guy to her left said, "I would've gotten you a beer. You should've said something."

Reese lifted a shoulder in a mini-shrug and accepted the cup Adam held out to her. She pointed at Adam. "He's the artist who drew my tattoo."

Everyone turned to look at him. "Hi."

Three people started talking at once about what they wanted him to draw. He held up a hand. "I'll be in the living room in a little bit to do more tattoos. My hand needs a rest." He grabbed Reese's hand and tugged her from the group. "Can I talk to you a minute?"

"Sure." She smiled at everyone as he led her away from the kitchen.

He pulled her back toward his bedroom, but didn't enter. He continued to hold her hand, even though he no longer had a reason. "Sorry about that. Hunter needs my help, but I don't want you to feel left out."

"I'm fine. There are a lot of friendly people here. Do what you need to do." She drank the beer he poured her.

"I'm glad you came."

"So am I."

"I'll be around. Just holler if you need any-thing." He looked around for Free and found him chatting with Lisa. "You know Hunter. And that tall guy over there wearing the brown pin-striped suit? That's Free. He's my other friend."

"I've seen him at the shop before. He was dressed like Sherlock Holmes." She laughed at whatever image popped in her head of Free.

"Today he's Doctor Who. If you need some-thing and can't find me, go to them."

"I'll be fine." She slid her hand from his grasp.

He didn't want to let go, but he'd promised Hunter some help. At least for a little while. Then the rest of his night would be spent with Reese.

~

Reese wandered through the apartment with her beer and talked with a roomful of strangers. After about an hour, Hunter and his band started playing music, and they were good. Although Reese worried about feeling weird at the party, she was having fun. Everyone was friendly. It was probably the free-flowing alcohol, but Reese didn't care.

Adam checked on her repeatedly. He was cute, the way he worried about whether she was having a good time. While she talked with some guys, she felt Adam watching her, so she smiled at him to let him know she was fine. Even as the conversation around her continued, she stared at Adam drawing on another woman. She couldn't tell what the design was, but it was small.

The woman squealed and kissed Adam on the cheek. He shied away from her touch, which gave Reese some satisfaction. She enjoyed the way Adam had touched her when he'd drawn her tattoo, and she didn't like the idea that other people would get the same treatment. She wanted to believe that what they'd shared was special, that she was special. When they were alone in his room, it was easy to believe.

But now, out here, in the middle of a party, surrounded by a crowd, it should've been harder to feel, but it was still there. Every time their eyes met, a spark of desire zinged through her, and she didn't think it was a one-way thing.

The music picked up and she winked at Adam. She wanted to dance. She moved back to the living room, where Hunter and his band played. Kicking off her shoes, Reese raised her arms and danced to the rhythm. The vibrations of the floor hummed through her. It was nearing midnight and the partiers joined in on the makeshift dance floor. Drunk bodies crashed into hers, laughing and drinking.

Suddenly hands were on her hips. She turned to find Adam behind her, barely an inch between them.

"You okay?"

"I'm having a blast. Dance with me."

"Are you drunk?"

She shook her head. "No, but I'm getting there. How about you?"

"Working on it."

His hands still held her hips, not confining, just holding. She began to sway again, and Hunter switched up to a slow song. Reese didn't recognize it, but it was beautiful and sexy. She wrapped her arms around Adam's neck and waited to see if he would pull away. He didn't, so she nudged closer.

Their bodies melded into one. Adam's hands slid around to her lower back. She laid her head on his shoulder.

"This is a mistake," he whispered in her ear.

"Says who?"

"We both know it. We shouldn't do this."

"Shouldn't, huh? But you want to?"

"You know I do. You're making me crazy, dancing in this skimpy dress and talking with all these other guys. It's like you're trying to make me jealous."

"If you're not interested, it wouldn't be possible to make you jealous. You wouldn't care."

"But I do."

"I didn't dress like this to make you jealous."

"Then why?"

"I did it because I thought you would like it."

"I do."

The music stopped and everyone around them began chattering. It took a moment for her to realize that they were getting ready to count down to midnight.

A drumroll sounded behind her and everyone began chanting, "Ten, nine, eight..."

Reese stared up into Adam's eyes, wanting to pull him closer, but needing him to make the first move. He stared back, his chest rising and touching hers in the process.

"Seven, six, five..."

His fingers flexed at her waist. She licked her lips and left them slightly parted in invitation.

"Four, three, two..."

Celebration rang out around them as Adam's mouth came down on hers. She plastered her body against his and let him lead. His mouth was hot and wet and his tongue slid past her lips. She heard nothing more as Adam filled all of her senses.

She was buzzed and the alcohol should've dulled everything, but it hadn't. Each of her cells was alive and alert. Reese's body lined up perfectly with Adam's. His hard-on pressed against her, so she ground her hips.

More. She wanted more.

He pulled away and stared at her. His pupils were huge and he panted. For a second, she thought for sure he'd continue to back up, out of her embrace, away from her body. Then the corners of his mouth quirked up and he came at her again. He kissed her like he owned her.

This time, when he pulled her close, his hands drifted over her ass and squeezed. The material of the short dress bunched, and a draft hit her upper thighs, cooling the heat Adam created. His mouth left hers and he kissed her neck, her ears, across the top of her chest. His fingers traced the edges of the tattoo he'd drawn hours ago, and she wanted nothing more than for him to pull the top of her dress down and use his fingers all over the rest of her body.

He ran his hands down her arms until they met hers. Then he stepped away, tugging her with him. "Let's go to my room."

He didn't wait for her to respond. He just continued to pull her through the crowd of people who were laughing and kissing and clinking plastic cups of beer. He plowed through the door to his room and stopped. "Shit."

"What?" She peered around his shoulder and saw a mountain of coats and jackets piled on his bed.

"Why did people think this would be a good idea?"

She shrugged. "Hunter told me to bring my coat in here."

"I'm gonna kill him." He released her hand and scooped up an armful of coats. "Wait here."

Reese watched him leave the room, but rather than listen to his directions, she, too, grabbed a stack and followed him. The quicker they got things moved, the faster they would be alone. And right now, her entire body screamed to be alone with Adam.

She struggled out into the short hallway with the coats and crashed into Adam. He must've run to another room to get back this quickly.

"I'll take these. Let Hunter deal with people getting their shit." He spun and she realized he was dumping the coats on the bed in the room across the hall.

At least he was keeping it simple. She returned to the room to grab more, but Adam was on her heels. He hauled the remaining coats and simply said, "Sit. Relax. I'll be right back."

Reese stood awkwardly, not quite sure what she should do. Get undressed? Fix her makeup and hair? Lie down on the bed? Before she could decide, the door thumped closed behind her and she heard the snick of the lock.

She inhaled deeply and turned to Adam.

He closed the distance and said, "Now, where were we?"

"I believe we were making a mistake," she murmured as his lips came down on hers.

CHAPTER TEN

This was not the slow and patient, almost hesitant kiss they'd shared last week. This wasn't even the crush of lips in the living room minutes ago. This kiss was hot and hard and wet and fast. Their mouths clashed and their hands couldn't move quickly enough to touch each other.

Reese yanked at Adam's T-shirt while he kissed along her collarbone, tugging at the crisscross straps with his teeth. His hands were under her dress, drifting higher, and he obviously didn't want to waste time worrying about straps. Her fingers barely grazed his abdomen when his hand stroked her.

She gasped. He paused. She was set on fire with need for him. She fisted his T-shirt and pulled it over his head, which meant he had to release his grip on her. That was as far as she got, though, because he moved back in, pulling the top of her dress down to expose her boobs. The straps slid off her right shoulder and restricted the movement of that arm, but she didn't care because Adam's mouth was hot on her nipple.

He bit and sucked and soothed. All she could do was hold his head with her free hand. He shoved the hem of her dress up as he walked her back to the bed and pushed her down. She attempted to wiggle around to unzip and remove the dress, but Adam covered her body, kissing and touching her, and she could no longer think.

Adam moved down her body, caressing her as he went. He shoved her thighs wide and ran his fingers over the lace of her panties. She raised her hips, inviting him to take them off, but she heard a tear.

Her eyes bugged. "Did you just rip my underwear?"

He smirked.

"They were my favorite pair."

"I'll buy you new ones." He stroked his long fingers over her slowly. "I can't promise not to do that again, though."

She never thought a guy ruining her panties would be sexy, but this definitely was.

Adam leaned forward and kissed her neck again. "God, you're so wet."

"For you. You do this to me," she whispered.

He answered with a groan. His thumb pressed against her clit and he slid two fingers into her. Her hips bucked up. She needed release. Tension coiled in her and her nerves were on edge. She wanted to hold this feeling, but she wanted to speed to the end and explode all at once.

Again he sucked on her nipples, flicking his tongue in rhythm to what his hand was doing. All she could do was hold his head close, wishing his hair was long enough to grip.

Her orgasm spiked and she came with a long moan. As Adam pulled back, she tried to reach up, but her arm was still trapped by the stupid straps. She never had this problem with a T-shirt.

She struggled to sit up. "Can you help me get this off now? I feel like I'm in a straitjacket."

He chuckled and the low sound shot through her. While her hands fought to find the zipper in the back, she leaned forward and kissed him, sucking his lower lip into her mouth. She sank her teeth in just enough to stop his laughing. He hissed, but didn't pull away. His arms snaked behind her and unzipped the dress.

The bunched-up material eased away from her, and Adam pulled it free. She shimmied to get it off her body and she sat naked in front of him. He stared until she pointed at him. "It'd be nice if you took your clothes off, too."

She scooted back on the bed and watched as he undid his jeans and shoved them down. His boxer briefs were tight enough to outline his erection, which turned her on more. She hopped up on her knees and kissed his chest, trailing her wet mouth across his smooth skin. Like he had done to her, she flicked her tongue over his brown nipple as she slid her fingers inside his waistband.

His heart thumped against her lips as her fingers circled him and stroked. He was thick and hot. The thought of him being inside her set off another round of pulsing need. She ran her hand over the length of his smooth, taut skin. She'd made him as hard as he'd made her wet. She felt great satisfaction in that.

Adam pushed her gently back on the mattress and then leaned over to the nightstand. He put a condom on and crawled back over her body. Reese wrapped her legs around his hips and said, "Now, Adam."

He grabbed himself and rubbed against her, sending jolts of pleasure every time he bumped her clit. She was closer than she thought, but she wanted more. When he finally pushed into her, she sighed with relief.

Adam buried his face in her neck with a groan. He didn't move, so she enjoyed having him pressed against her, feeling all of his skin gliding along hers.

He began to move, in slow, patient strokes, re-straining himself. Reese dug her heels in his ass and pushed up. The movement was enough to spur him into action. His pace picked up and he braced his arms on the sides of her head. As much as she wanted to continue to look up at his face, fierce and tense with pleasure, her eyes fluttered closed in her own enjoyment.

Adam reared up and grabbed her ankle, pulling her leg high to rest on his shoulder. The change in angle along with his hard thrusts made her second orgasm greater than the first. Behind her closed eyes, she saw shooting stars brighter than the one she wore on her chest. Her muscles tensed and air locked in her lungs as she rode the wave of her inner muscles contracting and pulling at Adam.

With a hand gripping her hip and another still like a vise on her ankle, he drove into her. "Ah, fuck," he murmured as his flesh slapped against hers. Then he groaned and held still again before releasing her leg and collapsing on her.

They both lay there, panting, and the sounds of the party began to filter back to Reese. She'd never had sex with a house full of people on the other side of a door. She giggled. "You left the party to have sex."

Adam rolled off her. "So did you."

"But it's your party. Aren't people going to look for you?"

He lifted a shoulder. "They haven't yet." He wrapped an arm around her waist and pulled her close. She interlocked her fingers with his. They both stared at their joined hands. She loved the contrast he brought to her life.

"That dress should've come with a warning. Do not wear unless you want to be fucked senseless."

She swallowed hard. The dress. They'd just had amazing sex, and all he mentioned was the dress. She swallowed again before trying to speak. "Well, it's Julie's dress. I'll be sure to tell her."

His long fingers traced a pattern across her ribs. She imagined him drawing on her again.

"Maybe you should keep it."

"In case you didn't notice, it's not really my style." She kept her eyes closed and tilted her head away from him.

"It was definitely your style tonight." He nuzzled closer to her, his breath fluttering at the fine hairs on her neck.

She should take the compliment for what it was. He thought she looked hot. At least for tonight. In a borrowed dress. It was what she'd wanted, for Adam to notice her, to act on the attraction she knew he felt. All it took was for her to dress like she was a different person.

Why exactly did she think that would be a good idea?

Because now she was lying in bed next to him, after having some great sex, and feeling like she wanted to cry. She blinked a few times to clear her eyes before sitting up. "I should get going."

"You can't drive. You've had too much to drink."

"I'll be fine."

He sat up and held her wrist. "Spend the night. It'll be safer. You'll be sober, and so will all the other drivers on the road." He lowered his head and stared into her eyes. "Please."

The urge to cover herself burned through her under his careful scrutiny. "Can I borrow some different clothes? I don't want to sleep in the dress, and people are probably going to come looking for their coats. I'd prefer not to be seen naked."

His eyebrows wrinkled together. "Sure." He got off the bed and rummaged through his dresser. He tossed her a pair of sweatpants and a T-shirt before pulling on a pair of shorts.

She dressed quickly and scooted back on the bed. "If you need to go check on your guests, I understand."

He glanced over his shoulder at the closed door and then back at her.

She didn't wait for a response. She turned to her side and pulled the blanket over her. He made some noise behind her and then she heard the *click* of the door.

Adam had been right from the get-go. This was a mistake. She should've listened to him. They had a good thing going, and now she didn't know if she could go back.

THE SUN GLARING THROUGH HIS WINDOW WOKE Adam the following morning. He shivered and reached across the bed, only to find it empty. Reese was gone. He had no idea what had gone wrong last night, but he knew something had. The sex had been good—great, even—so it wasn't that.

Something bothered Reese and he thought by giving her some space last night, she'd get over it and be okay. Instead, when he came back to the room after telling everyone where to find their coats, she was asleep. He reached for his phone and sent her a text.

Why'd you leave?

He kept the phone in his hand and dozed while waiting for an answer. He was right yesterday and every other day when he looked at her and knew that sleeping with her would be a mistake. She embodied complication.

Your apartment is cold. And you snore.
Everything okay?
Yeah. I need to get stuff ready to launch our campaign. Need to take advantage of time off.
Anything I can help with?
Nope. I got it covered.

Although she hadn't said anything wrong, he

felt like she was distant. He couldn't put his finger on why her texts bothered him or why they didn't quite sound like her, but he knew.

I'll be at the shop if you need me.
Ok
Talk to you later?
Sure

He tossed his covers off and climbed out of bed. Maybe he was reading too much into everything. Maybe she really was just busy today.

Last night didn't have to be some momentous thing between them. They'd both been drinking and things got out of hand. If she hadn't been wearing that damn dress, he never would've made a move.

Liar. He remembered the sight of her in his sweats, rolled multiple times at the waist to stay up, and he'd wanted her all over again. He drove to the shop to help his mom with organizing the back room and clearing stuff out. Although the shop was open, it was never busy because of the holiday. It had become tradition for them to clean out the stockroom on New Year's Day. Plus, it got him out of the bulk of cleaning from the party.

He got to the shop and his mom already had boxes stacked behind the register. He started sorting through the random toys and back issues of comics. Every five minutes, he thought he felt his phone vibrate, so he pulled it out.

"Who are you waiting for?"

"Huh?"

"You've checked your phone at least ten times in as many minutes."

He shrugged. "I thought Reese might call."

She buried her face in another box, but he caught her smile. "So you like her?" she asked without looking up.

"We're friends."

"I've never seen you check your phone that often for Free."

He sighed. Of course she was right; she usually was.

"For what it's worth, I like her, too."

"We're friends and business partners. That's all."

"You keep telling yourself that." She pulled some action figures out and kicked the now empty box aside. "I was thinking maybe we should get some shelves over here just for the toys. I think these will sell if we have them out. What do you think?"

"Sounds good." He was too preoccupied to consider toys. All he could think about was the repercussions of not keeping his dick in his pants last night. He hadn't wanted to hurt Reese, but he didn't even know what he'd done wrong.

He kept replaying the night in his head. He re-membered telling her that it was a mistake, and she brushed it aside because they both wanted it. She knew the score. It looked like he'd have to have one of those stupid conversations where they needed to go back to being strictly in the friend zone. If she was able to do it with her ex-boyfriend, she should have no problem doing it with him. They hadn't dated and they only slept together once, while they were drunk.

Not really drunk. It was sad that he was looking for excuses for his behavior.

He pulled out his phone and called Reese's number. Of course, it went to voice mail. She was dodging him.

"Hey, Reese. I just wanted to talk about last night, make sure things are really okay with us. We were both drinking, and like I said last night, we shouldn't have done that—not that it wasn't great. It was. I just don't want to complicate things. Let me know when you're free to work on the next story together. Call me."

When they took a break for lunch, he finally got a text from Reese.

I told you we're fine. We had some great sex. So what? I'll send you the next story as soon as it's done.

He wanted to hear her voice, not just read some words on the screen. It was easy for her to lie like that. She was a writer after all.

She wanted more space. He could give her that. Space would give them both perspective to clear their minds and recoup. Then they could get back to normal.

CHAPTER ELEVEN

Reese stared at the screen and couldn't believe her eyes. Their campaign went live less than two days ago. She posted synopses of the first stories and a couple of Adam's pictures. Then she and Julie hit social media and begged people to spread the word.

This, however, was unimaginable. She blinked and rubbed her eyes. Not only had they met their goal within the first forty-eight hours, but they had far exceeded it. Julie called her at the ass-crack of dawn and told her to get online. She still held her phone, albeit not by her ear.

Julie had started prattling on about offering additional packages that would include things like signed artwork or rough drafts. Reese just hit the end button and disconnected. She couldn't wrap her head around this, much less think about expanding.

She stood and went to the kitchen, where her mom already had coffee brewing. After a dose of caffeine, it would make more sense.

Her mom came around the corner from the

bathroom. "Hey, honey. What are you doing up so early?" She squinted at her. "Or are you just getting to bed?"

"Up. Julie called. My project is a success."

"Already? I thought you said it would take weeks to find enough investors or whatever." She walked around Reese and filled her cup.

"I thought it would. I'm not sure how it happened. That's next on my list. Right now, I'm just taking a minute to enjoy the fact that all the worrying and obsessing was worth it." She sipped her coffee and smiled. While she still had some concerns that people would be disappointed in the final product, overall, she felt relieved.

With her cup in hand, she went back to her computer and Googled herself as well as the comic. "Oh, crap." Her hand flew to her mouth. Somehow, some of the biggest geek and pop culture sites had picked up her story from social media. She was all over the Internet.

Her phone rang. "Hello?"

"You hung up on me."

"Yeah."

"Are you done freaking now?"

"Kind of. We're everywhere. Have you seen this?"

"Of course. Now that people know who we are, we need to expand. We don't have time to mess around."

In her usual efficient nature, Julie had a list of things prepared. She was going to handle the updates to backers and the organization of the additional packages. Now that they had their funding, they could play around with other ideas.

Unfortunately, all of them put Reese squarely with Adam. She'd successfully avoided him since the party. Julie had asked how the dress worked and Reese barely prevented herself from crying. It had been a stupid move. One that she almost regretted. Being the good friend that she was, Julie let it drop.

"I need some more background for the next update. People are going to want to know how far along you are, how you're developing things, where Adam gets his inspiration. Those are all posts that people will eat up. We want to keep our momentum going." She paused. "Are you listening?"

"Yeah. More information, behind-the-scenes stuff." Reese's stomach flip-flopped. Behind the scenes meant exposing her interactions with Adam. She'd only gotten this far because of his help. Bouncing ideas off each other was what worked. She just didn't think she was ready to face him. "I'll get you a post by the end of the day and I'll send you Adam's info so you can ask him."

"So you're still hiding, huh?"

"Not hiding. Just reassessing."

"Liar."

"Whose side are you on?"

"Yours. Always yours. He's an idiot if he doesn't want you."

"Thanks. I'll get this done and I should have the next synopsis for you later. We're in good shape." As she spoke to Julie, she sent Adam an e-mail with the script of the next comic. Her message was professional and to the point without being bitchy.

She invited his input. And she really wanted it; she just didn't want to be face-to-face to get it.

Then she went to work on the synopsis for the story she sent Adam. A half hour later, just as she was settling in for a nap, she got a text from Adam. **This looks pretty good. I have some ideas. Free tomorrow?**

Damn. She couldn't catch a break. She needed him to continue, which meant that she couldn't let him know how hurt she was. She didn't even know why she was hurt. What had she thought? That if Adam hit on her, took her to bed, that he would fall instantly in love with her? No, she had been testing his attraction, making sure it hadn't been all one-sided or in her head.

He was attracted to her—at least when she looked like Julie. She, however, couldn't be Julie. She couldn't sustain that look, not that she wanted to. At least she knew where she stood with him. Time to put it away and go back to being productive.

No matter how she looked at it, they were better together. She shot back a text. **I'm working until two. You want me to come to the shop?**

See you then. Bring me a magic coffee?

She couldn't help but smile. **Of course.**

Reese curled up under her blanket and closed her eyes. She had a little over a day to figure out how to work with Adam and not think about him naked and kissing her.

Sure, no problem.

ADAM SPED THROUGH THE WORK HE HAD TO DO AND hoped that they wouldn't have too many customers. Of course that was bad for his mom's business, but he needed time with Reese. He needed to be able to talk with her without a million interruptions. He would've suggested meeting at her apartment, or even his, but since she'd e-mailed the last story to him, he didn't think she'd be receptive to the idea of being alone with him.

It was probably a good idea for them not to be alone together. He wasn't very good at controlling himself. For days, every time he closed his eyes, all he saw was Reese's body, bare but for his mark tattooed on her chest. No matter how he tried to replace those images, nothing worked. He was resigned to fantasizing about her indefinitely.

After a late lunch, he began sketching out ideas for the next story, marking where he had questions. When the bell over the door chimed, he was so engrossed in drawing that he didn't even realize it was Reese.

"I'm not sure I like that look," she said. As she approached the desk, she reached out to hand him a coffee.

He smiled. He'd totally forgotten he'd asked her to bring him one. He'd only asked as a test to make sure they were okay.

"The story's good. I'm not sure where you're going with it, though. It seems darker than the earlier issues." He sipped the special brew she'd made for him.

"Before we get into that, I need to update you on the campaign. Have you checked it at all?"

He shook his head. "It's your project. I'm in charge of artwork, not financing."

"We funded our goal. In less than two days."

"Okay."

As she shimmied out of her jacket, she said, "That's not okay. It's amazing. We're all over the Internet. People love the concept. They're raving about your art."

He paused mid-sip. "My art?"

"I uploaded a few images for people to see. We're nobodies. Why would anyone offer us money without an idea whether the finished product will be any good? I gave them a sneak peek."

"It's fine. I didn't realize it would be posted already."

She huffed. "You really *haven't* looked at any-thing, have you?"

"I'm in this for the art. I don't much care about the rest." He set his cup on the counter, away from the sketches. "Ready to talk about this?"

"Not yet. Julie thinks we need to expand our offerings, which would generate more money."

"I thought this was about your grade, not money."

"It's about both." She waved a hand. "Anyway, Julie will be e-mailing you with details of the stuff she'd like you to do. It's up to you to decide what you agree to." She stopped talking and for a minute, just stared at him.

Questions swirled behind her eyes, and he feared what might pop out when she next opened her mouth, so he tried to steer the conversation to safe regions of their friendship. "It seems like you

have Gunner pulling away from Alexis in this issue. I thought you wanted to get them together."

"So did I. But that's not where the story
led me."

Crap. So much for avoiding this conversation.
She had their relationship reflected in her characters. With his luck, she'd start killing people off,
starting with Gunner. "How can he be a mentor if
he runs away?"

"He needs a reason to stay." Her response was
barely a whisper.

As much as he didn't want to have this conversation, he pushed forward. "We need to talk about
New Year's Eve."

She shook her head and blinked rapidly. "We're
fine. We were both drinking, I wasn't looking like
myself, and it made it easy for things to be different between us. I get it. It was a onetime thing.
I'm not your type. Julie has her dress back, and I'm
once again in cargo pants and T-shirts. You're
safe."

He fucking hated it when women were cryptic.
He took a second to try to decode what she said.
"Do you think I slept with you because of the
dress?"

"You did."

He pinched the bridge of his nose before
looking at her again. "Don't get me wrong. You
were fucking hot in that dress, but I don't ran-
domly pick up hot women to sleep with. I had sex
with you because *you* turn me on."

Her face filled with confusion. Her jaw set
tight. "Then why do you keep saying we're a
mistake?"

"Because as a couple, we would be."

"You make zero sense. We like each other. We laugh and have a great time together. You just got done telling me that I turn you on. Where's the problem?" She crossed her arms.

There was no pleasant way to say this. No matter what, he was going to sound like an asshole. "I can't date you because you're white."

As soon as the words left his mouth, a customer came in. The worst damn timing. He greeted the customer, moving as far from Reese as he could. The words he'd left dangling between them wouldn't be enough. He knew he needed to explain. Luckily, the customer was only picking up his preorder so he was gone quickly.

When Adam turned back to Reese, her cheeks were pink and she glared at him. "Did you honestly just say that you can't date me because I'm white? Your *mom* is white."

Her fire had a bizarre effect on him. He was both angry and getting turned on. "I'm aware."

Before he could continue explaining, she launched at him again. "How can you define people by their race and accuse me of being naïve? When I invited you to my game night, did I tell you about my friends by describing their race?" She angled her head and stiffened the tone of her voice. "It's Lee's apartment. He's a big black guy. Chris is my Korean American friend, but his girlfriend, Kim, looks like she belongs on the Swedish volleyball team. And let's not forget my Puerto Rican ex-boyfriend."

She had him there. Game night was like the United Nations of friends.

She jabbed a finger in the air at him. "No. I told you who they were, what they did for a living. I judge people by how they act and how they treat me, regardless of skin color."

"So do I. You don't understand what it's like to get those looks."

Her arms flailed at him. "You're right, Adam. I'll never fear for my life when a cop stops me. But don't assume that I don't know what it's like to be discriminated against. By virtue of not being born with a dick, people often assume I am *less than*—less intelligent and less capable."

He sighed. This was all so wrong. "I don't mean that." He swallowed hard. "Even your mom gave me a worried look when I was at your place watching a movie with you in the dark."

She took a step closer. "My mom didn't look at you with distrust because you're black. She looked at you that way because you're a man. She distrusts all men because she was abused. But she trusts me to make better choices than she did."

The door opened again and Bonnie walked through. She took in the sight of the two of them, agitated and on edge. No way could he have this conversation in front of his mom. He pulled his car keys from his pocket and shoved Reese's jacket at her.

"I'll be back in a little bit," he said to his mom. Then he grabbed Reese's hand and dragged her across the store and out the door to his car. He should've put on his own damn coat. It was fucking freezing out. He unlocked the door and opened it for Reese.

She stared at him with her arms crossed, still

holding her jacket.

"I'd like to finish our conversation. Please get in."

She climbed into his car, and he ran around and got behind the wheel. He started the engine and turned up the heat. Reese slid her arms into her jacket while he shivered.

"I'm not trying to hurt you. I just want you to understand."

"Well, I don't." She crossed her arms again. "I think it would've been easier to keep believing you weren't attracted to me. That you liked me only when I was dressed up like Julie. Because at least then, I had some control. I could change if I really wanted to, not that I do. But you're holding some-thing against me that I have zero control over."

"It's not you." She snorted and he stared out the windshield at the front of the shop. "I was born into an interracial family. I obviously get my skin color from my dad."

"You never talk about him."

"He's not a big part of my life. He lives in Ohio now. My parents loved each other. I remember that when I was little. They smiled and laughed and were happy. But I also remember the way people would stare at us, the comments they made. My dad couldn't handle it, so he left."

From the corner of his eye, he saw Reese lean closer and open her mouth and then snap it shut again.

"He's not a bad guy. He always supported me. He gave me the life lessons he'd thought I'd need living as a black man. He didn't move to Ohio until I graduated high school. He was around, but

I never felt like I'd be really close to him because I'm a lot like my mom." There. He said it. It wasn't nearly as bad as he'd thought it would be. He stole a peek at Reese.

Her eyes narrowed again. "So even though you like me and you're attracted to me, you won't date me because people might say mean shit?"

The incredulity in her voice irked him. She still didn't understand, just like he thought.

"No. People are going to say shit about me and I know that."

"Are you worried I can't handle it?"

Was he? Sure. But he knew better than to say that. She'd finally calmed down enough that smoke stopped streaming from her ears. That kind of honesty would bring it all back. "I don't think I can handle people saying shit about us. And if I can't handle it, you'll end up getting hurt."

She laid a hand on his arm, warming his chilled skin. He turned to face her. She licked her lips and all he could think about was kissing her.

"So, if I'm understanding right, you're afraid you're like your dad. That you'll run from happiness because outside forces make it hard."

That was it in a nutshell. He gave her a stiff nod.

"I wish you could understand that you have choices, too. By your way of thinking, I shouldn't date anyone because I might be like my mom and choose someone who'll beat me. We get to choose who we are, Adam. It's sad that you don't know that." She gave his arm a little pat and opened the car door. "Shoot me a text when you have the sketches done and we'll talk."

He watched her walk through the parking lot without a glance back. She wasn't running away or cutting him off. She still wanted to work with him.

What about when the comics were done? Then what? Would they just not see each other again?

She'd get over it. If she could continue to be friends and hang out with her ex-boyfriend, surely one night of sex wouldn't ruin everything for them. He turned the key in the ignition, but continued to stare at the store. His mom would ask questions. He wasn't sure he was ready to face her.

He shoved out of the car and ran back into the store. His mom stood behind the register and glanced behind him. "Where's Reese?"

"She left."

"Are you two fighting?"

"Kind of." He walked to his desk and gathered his papers. He glanced over the sketches he'd done of Alexis as Lyrid with Gunner watching her. Adam hadn't gotten the chance to tell Reese why he thought the story was going in the wrong direction.

"Business or personal?"

"Huh?"

"Your disagreement. Was it over the comic or was it personal?"

Although the question made sense, Adam had never thought about them being separate. "Personal." *Very.*

"Want to talk about it?"

"Not much to say. I did something stupid and although I apologized, I don't know if we can go back."

His mom came close and rubbed a hand across

his shoulders. "Are you sure you want to go back?"

"We have to."

"Why?"

He slid away from his mother's touch. "I don't want to end up like you and Dad."

"What?"

"Reese got mad because I won't date her because she's white."

His mother, usually calm and laid-back, hauled off and smacked the back of his head. He winced and rubbed at the spot.

"What was that for?"

"Talking stupid. I raised you better than that. You're going to walk away from a beautiful girl who really cares about you because of the color of her skin?"

He closed his eyes and inhaled, preparing to explain himself. Again. "I don't have a problem with the color of her skin. If I wasn't attracted to her, I wouldn't have slept with her."

From the glare he received now, he realized that wasn't the right thing to say either. He took another step back in case another swat was headed his way.

"What does any of that have to do with me and your father?"

"What if I'm not strong enough?"

"What do you mean?"

"I'm afraid that I won't be able to handle the looks and comments, derisive remarks. That I'll run away like Dad did." He hung his head. He knew his parents loved him and that should've been enough. He'd never felt the need to discuss these fears.

His mom cupped his cheek and forced him to look up. "Your father was far from a great husband. Things didn't work out between us, but it had nothing to do with race."

"Don't lie to me, Mom. I remember him getting mad that people would look at us funny at the park. I remember you trying to talk him down."

"And maybe that was my mistake. I didn't want him to make a scene because I didn't want to give anyone that kind of hold on my life. I'd hoped you were too young to understand. Your father is strong. He'd take on a whole army to protect you, so you could have whatever life you want." Her eyes filled with tears. "Your dad and I split up because it wasn't working between us."

He took a step back. "I get that. That's what you've said my whole life, but the undercurrent has always been there, too."

"It doesn't matter. Surround yourself with people who care about you. Do you get strange looks for being friends with Hunter? Or Free? Because let's face it, that boy is weird."

He laughed and so did she. A few tears fell while she laughed. Free *was* weird, and no one ever gave a second thought to who his best friends were.

Their laughter stopped and his mom sobered. "People are going to be assholes. Nothing you can do about it. Just live your life. I do." Then she smiled and walked to the back room.

Adam stared at the sketches for the comic. His mother offered good advice, as usual. He couldn't argue with it, but he didn't know how to do it either.

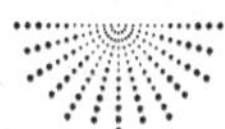

CHAPTER TWELVE

More than two weeks flew by, and Adam still had no clue what he was doing. He and Reese worked mostly via e-mail. She sent him pieces of the story and he responded with comments and ideas. This comic had gone almost nowhere since she first e-mailed it to him and they fought in the shop. It was like they'd lost their mojo.

He was sure she felt it too. They didn't fight over the story direction; it just wasn't working. He sat in his room with pages spread across both desks. He stared at the images. No words appeared anywhere because the text kept changing.

The silence of his room pounded down on him. The one time he longed for Hunter to be here, making noise, playing music, he was nowhere to be found. He spun on his chair, trying to get comfortable, and he remembered his first kiss with Reese. They'd sat so close, the constant low-level hum of energy zapped between them.

There had been no way he could've *not* kissed her. But before the kiss, they were in sync. They worked seamlessly. More than anything, he missed having that with her. Business calls and texts and e-mails weren't cutting it.

And if he was being totally honest, he wanted more. More collaboration, more laughter, more kissing, more fucking. He missed everything about her, and he had no idea how the hell that happened.

Before he lost his nerve, he called her.

"What's up?" she answered, friendly enough.

"This isn't working."

"What's not?"

"This story. Bouncing ideas back and forth via e-mail. We finished the first comic in one night of working together at your apartment. We raced through another in one night at mine. We've wasted two weeks not getting anything right with this one." He held his breath and waited.

"What are you saying? You want out?"

"No." He nearly yelled and dialed it back. "No. I think we need to work in person. It's a lot more productive."

Silence met his suggestion.

"I also need your help with the stuff Julie wants. I'm not the writer. I have no idea what I'm doing. I can come to your place, or you can come here. Wherever you'd be more comfortable. This comic has the potential to be amazing and I don't want to fuck it up."

"Neither do I." Her sigh was quiet. "I'm free now. Is your apartment good, or are Hunter and company playing music?"

"I don't know where Hunter is, so here is fine. Unless…"

"Unless what?"

"Unless you won't be comfortable here alone with me."

She snickered. "We've already covered that. Since I'm still white, I have nothing to worry about. Be there soon."

Her comment stung, but he had it coming. He raced through the apartment, flipping on lights and making sure it was clean.

When Reese arrived, he met her outside with a permit for her to park. She followed him into the apartment silently. They went straight to his room, where she took off her jacket and hung it on the back of the chair he'd brought in for her. She scooted to be in front of one desk, leaving his stool by the other.

Clearly, she planned to keep her distance. "Work your magic, Adam. Where did we go wrong?" As she spoke, she scanned the pages in front of her.

"Gunner made contact with Lyrid in the last book, but you have him pulling back here. I don't know how much readers will be willing to put up with if they aren't given a reason."

Reese traced an image of Gunner with her finger. "He doesn't think he's good enough for her. Not as a friend, not as a mentor. So he pulls back."

"But you don't have that on the page. He's just being an asshole to her, and she doesn't know how to handle that."

Reese hopped in her seat, suddenly excited. "That's it. That's the problem. Gunner has already gotten her to accept her new powers. She needs to grow a pair. Push back at him for being an asshole. Fight for him."

She reached into a pocket and came up with a pencil. Then she started pushing papers around, and he fought the cringe as she made a mess. Finally, she just flipped a page over and began scribbling.

Adam wheeled his stool closer to see what she wrote, but her arms covered the words. He handed her a printed-out copy of their latest revision. She flipped through it and went back to her scribbles. Mumbling to herself, she said, "If we scrap page two, and move three later…"

He sat quietly and watched. This was the Reese he missed. She became engrossed in her story—their story—and he realized he didn't want it to end. She filled the page in her hand and thrust it at him. "Get started. I think this is right."

He read what she'd written. This was it. This was what had been missing for the last two weeks. He grabbed clean paper and started over, using the new text. He shifted some of the panels she had listed. When she saw, she poked at them and argued for her arrangement.

They argued, disagreed, and then compromised.

It all felt too simple.

For the next two hours, they went back and forth, creating story and images. As they worked, Reese relaxed and closed the distance between them, both the physical and the emotional. When they got to the last page, his hand was cramping, but a smile creased his face. Reese leaned over and drew a smiley face on the page where he worked.

"Some artistry."

She was still leaning across his desk. Over her shoulder, she said, "I know. Maybe you should frame it. Might make you a millionaire."

Her cocky grin completely undid him. He dropped his pencil and wrapped his hand around the back of her neck, drawing her closer. Hesitation never crossed his mind when he captured her mouth. He sank into her, feeling the comfort she offered, hoping she felt the same.

A hard hand slapped his chest and she shoved away. "What are you doing?"

He stared at her and said the first thing that came to mind. "Living my life."

"What the hell does that mean? Don't play games with me." She stood and snatched her jacket off the chair.

"I'm not playing."

"What do you expect?"

"How about you kiss me back?"

"Why? So that tomorrow you can come to the realization that I'm still white?"

"I don't care what color you are. I told you that before." Fear and longing stole through him.

"No. You said you wouldn't date me because I'm white. I don't plan to be your dirty little secret booty call."

He jumped back. "That's not what I'm looking for."

"I'll talk to you later. I thought this was a good idea, and for a while there, it was." She turned and walked away.

He chased after her and caught her at the front door. He slammed his palm against the wood to prevent her from opening it. Speaking to the back of her head, he said, "I've missed you over the last couple of weeks. I don't want this to stop. Maybe I should've said that before I kissed you again, but I couldn't help myself."

She didn't turn to respond, but kept her hand on the doorknob. "You want me to believe that you're suddenly okay with being an interracial couple? That people staring or commenting isn't going to bother you?"

"Yes. No. It's going to bother me, but I don't care."

"I wish I could believe you." Then she pushed back against him and fled out the door.

Fuck. How was he supposed to fix this? In his head, it made sense. She was supposed to be in his arms, happy that he'd unfucked himself. Thrilled that he wanted to be with her.

But she hadn't said she didn't want to be with him, just that she didn't believe him. He'd have to figure out how to make her believe.

REESE RACED OUT OF ADAM'S HOUSE SO FAST THAT she skidded on the frozen ground on the way to her car. Emotions boiled through her, and she didn't know what to do. She knew coming here would be a mistake, but she couldn't help herself. The fact that not only had Adam asked her, but also that he recognized how well they worked together, forced her to come. She also figured it would be a good test for herself. She needed to know if she was able to work productively with him without wanting to strip him.

As she waited for her car to warm up, she looked back at the apartment. The hours she'd just spent there were great. She loved everything about being with Adam, including his surprise kiss. When his lips met hers, she wanted nothing more than to wrap herself around him.

But his words of fear echoed through her head.

The heat rattled to life. She took one last look at the building. Did she just run away from something great? He said he wanted her. That was all she'd wanted from him two weeks ago. Maybe he'd just needed time to come to terms with how he felt. It wasn't like he was the first emotionally stunted guy she'd known.

Throwing the car into drive, she pulled away. She couldn't sit there all night playing guessing games. On her way home, she half-expected Adam to call or text. That's what a guy was supposed to do if he wanted a girl.

Her phone remained silent all night. The following morning, she lay awake in bed, dreading getting up for class. The last semester of college had to be the worst. But she needed to move because she had to meet with her adviser about her senior project. Everything was on target, and she had little to worry about for that.

Even if Adam backed out, she still had three completed comics. It was more than most people were producing. Of course, she'd still have to write a paper about the entire experience and whether she thought crowd funding was a viable way to publish comics, but that was a no-brainer. It all boiled down to developing a quality team.

Adam was part of her quality team. She really wanted them to figure this shit out. When she opened the apartment door to head to school, a paper was taped to the front. A page from her comic. She tore it off the door and read. No, not a page from her comic, but her characters. Definitely Adam's drawing.

She read the text. It was his writing, too. A simple text box that said **Behind the scenes with Lyrid and Gunner—For your eyes only**. She remembered the first time she'd handed him a story. Now the man was not only acting strange, but he was making fun of her.

Lyrid was different, though. She was smaller, not as busty, and her top was different. The neckline scooped low without showing cleavage, like a tank top. On her left shoulder the shooting star that Adam had drawn on Reese peeked out from under the collar and the strap of the shirt.

It was beautiful, but she had no idea what this was supposed to mean. She ran down to her car and when she got behind the wheel, she found another picture. Staring at the sketch of Lyrid and Gunner, standing side by side, she tried to figure out what was different, but she couldn't quite put her finger on it. She laid the paper on the seat beside her and saw the note that read, "You really should lock your car."

As if someone would want to steal this piece of crap. She drove to school trying to figure out what Adam was doing. She hoped he didn't want to change the entire look of the characters at this point. Lyrid was looking more like what she'd wanted early in the process, but the first three books were done. She didn't want to go back and redo them.

After she met with her adviser, who was duly impressed with both the campaign and the quality of the stories, Reese got a text from Adam.

Didn't want to seem like a stalker following you to school, so here's the next panel.

Then he sent a photo of the drawing. Even without words on the page, she could tell that Gunner and Lyrid were arguing. Gunner was reaching for Lyrid's mask to pull it off. The mask was stretched to reveal a hint of her face her face.

What are you doing? She texted back, but got no response.

She went through her classes, and when she got back home, Adam was sitting on the steps waiting for her. "You didn't answer my text."

"I'm not good with words. So I finished the rest of the panels." He looked like hell, like he hadn't slept.

"Are you okay?"

"Not really." He handed her the last two pages.

In the first one, Gunner had removed Lyrid's mask and Reese's heart about stopped. She was staring at her own face. Only the back of Gunner's head was in the picture, but the hand that had torn away the mask still hovered near Lyrid's face. She'd know that hand anywhere. She looked up at Adam. Again, she asked, "What are you doing?"

He stood and slid the bottom page to the top. Gunner and Lyrid were in an embrace, lips almost touching, but it was Adam and Reese, not the characters they had created.

"You were right. I can't spend my life worrying about other people. Over the last couple of weeks, I realized that I don't want to live my life without you in it."

"We're still friends. I don't want you to pretend to be something that you're not. I learned my lesson."

"So have I."

She craned her neck to look at him. "I'm never going to be like Julie."

"I like the girl who gets excited to tell a story and has to think it out loud to make it work. The girl who asks so many questions she annoys the other gaming geeks. The girl who wears cargo pants with a pen or a pencil in different pockets. Where the hell would you stash a pen in that dress?" He stepped off the stairs, coming dangerously close to her.

When he invaded her space, she had a hard time thinking. "I don't know…"

"What's to know? Have you been happy these last couple of weeks?"

She shook her head.

His long fingers curled her hair around her ear, and his thumb traced the line of her jaw. "I tried to convince myself that being close to you and kissing you was a mistake. I don't know if it is, but I'm willing to take that chance over and over."

"What about being with a white girl and all the complications that brings?"

"White girl? All I see is a sexy woman standing

in front of me who I want to strip naked and trace every line of her body."

His words sent a tingle through her, turning her on. She imagined his hands touching her all over.

"What if—"

He cut her off with a kiss that melted her. His lips were strong and insistent, opening her mouth to him. His tongue glided into her, caressing her gently. As a moan rose in her throat, he pulled away.

"I don't want to give that up. I'm going to screw up and pull away when things get hard. I trust you to hold on and smack me when I'm being stupid. Can you do that?"

Reese let his words sink in. She loved his honesty, the fact that he didn't just try to take her on a date or to bed without addressing his fears. He was willing to face them. The least she could do was meet him halfway, because together, they were amazing. "I can try."

Adam slid his hand down her arm and interlocked his frozen fingers with hers. "If you like the new pictures of Lyrid, I'm willing to redraw the comics. I want you to know that I'm serious. The way you look doesn't matter. I was also thinking about giving Julie these sketches for her bonus material."

"No way. On both counts." Her voice was a little sharper than she intended. "First, we don't have to redo anything. Are you going to give up sleep? You already look like hell. If you're giving up sleep, I want it to be because you're with me, not because you're redrawing our comics." She softened her voice. "Second, I don't want anyone to have these sketches. This is us."

His fingers caressed her hand. "But I want the world to know that you're mine."

"Why don't we start with something simple, like a date out in public and work up to exhibitionism from there?"

He laughed loud and hard and she loved the sound, so she joined him. "I like a woman who sets goals. Let's get to work."

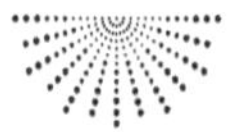

HIS NEW JAM

Sydney Peters shoved another spoonful of cereal in her mouth and stared at the calendar. Two weeks. That's all she had left to suffer through until marching band was over for the year. Two weeks of practice and drills and football games. Then she could pack up the fucking cymbals until next summer.

Her older sister Trisha came into the kitchen still in her robe. "Aren't you going to be late?"

"Whatever." Sydney slurped at her milk to prevent Trish from nagging again. They were both well aware she needed the scholarship the marching band gave her for school. It didn't mean Syd had to like it.

"I don't see what's so bad about band. You get to play the instrument you love. The music's not all bad. So the uniforms are a little dorky, but you look good on the field." Trisha poured herself a cup of coffee.

"I don't get to play the instrument I love. I play the damn cymbals. Just once I would like to be given an actual drum. I sucked it up last year as the new kid, waiting, thinking that at some point, as guys graduate, I could step up. Instead, it's this patronizing attitude. The drums are heavy. They'll be awkward. There are already other players waiting. But the worst is that I'm so good at the cymbals, they don't want to lose me." She dumped her bowl in the sink. "It's all bullshit. I don't even know why I need to finish school. I want to play. I don't need a degree to do that."

Trisha sighed the same way their mom always had. "We made a deal with Dad. You get to live with me in the city as long as you're in school."

"That was when I was underage. I'm twenty-one. I can live wherever I want."

Trish patted her arm. "But you don't want to let Dad down. Suck it up. Only another year and a half until graduation. Only a few weeks until you can forget about band for a while."

It annoyed her how well her sister knew her. Of course she wouldn't let their dad down. He'd decided the only way for them to have a good life was to go to college, like college could solve every problem. He held fast to the idea that if he had gone to college his life, and by extension their lives, would've been so much easier.

So she was in school, getting a graphic design degree that would be useless because all she wanted to do was play music.

But Trish did have a point: only a few weeks and she could say good-bye to being out in the cold, stomping on hard grass, pretending to enjoy herself during a football game. She tossed her backpack into her car and drove to the field. She shoved a hat on her head and grabbed her cymbals from the trunk. Just as she slammed the lid down, someone whistled at her.

Sydney's head popped up, ready to berate whatever asshole thought it was okay to catcall, when she saw her friend Emma running down the aisle of cars. She skidded to a halt in front of Sydney. "Whoa. You look ready to bite someone's head off."

"I thought you were some guy whistling at me."

"Lighten up. So what if I was? You look ready to commit bodily harm."

"I'm just extra cranky. It's cold and I want the season to be over. Plus, that tenor hasn't done his shit this week yet."

"What?"

"You know who I'm talking about. The tenor sax guy who hits on anything female. Every week since the summer, I can't walk by without him playing some song at me."

Emma smirked. "How do you know he's playing for you?"

They headed toward the field together. "He stands off to the side and waits for me to get within ten feet before playing a note. Trust me, he's flirting, in his own lame way."

Emma nudged her shoulder. "His name is Hunter. He's a huge flirt, but totally harmless. He's just having fun. He does it to make people smile. No one takes him seriously. As far as I know, he's never dated anyone from band. Plus, he's cute."

Emma had her there. They guy was cute, but even Syd knew he had a reputation for dating around a lot. She hadn't given him too much thought. Okay, that was a lie. Last season she'd crushed on him pretty hard, but he hadn't given her a second glance. She had no idea what had changed, but these past few months had been torturous.

She had no desire to waste her time on a fling with some guy who would toss her aside next week. "Does anyone ever flirt back? Maybe that's why he doesn't date anyone."

"Oh, no, plenty flirt back. It's a game to keep things fun. How could you not have caught on?"

"It wasn't included in band camp." Sydney wasn't quite sure what to do with that. They neared the mob of people who would turn into organized rows of musicians. Sure enough, tenor guy stood off to the side, staring in her direction even as he carried on a conversation with another sax player.

He said nothing as he brought his instrument up and played the first notes. Syd continued walking, trying to ignore him. She got a few feet past him when the notes of his song bounced through her mind and recognition hit. He was playing the damn Disney song "Let It Go."

Oh yeah, this guy was hilarious. So he thought she was an ice queen. He got close to the chorus and Syd paused midstride. Just as the ice queen accepted her fate, Sydney clashed her cymbals together and winked over her shoulder at Hunter. She was fine with being cold.

Holy shit. Hunter blinked and almost missed a note. Not only did Sydney Peters turn around and acknowledge that he was playing a song for her, she actually winked at him. Sure, it was more of a fuck-you wink than a flirtatious one, but it was still progress. He'd tried everything since summer to get her to react. The Pink Panther song didn't get her; neither did "Happy" or "Call Me Maybe." Although he thought he'd gotten an eye roll for that last one.

He liked to flirt with the band members. It kept things interesting when they spent a bunch of time marching and getting yelled at. It never went anywhere beyond fun conversation. There was something about Sydney that made him relentless. She always looked borderline miserable coming to practice. He thought maybe she wasn't a morning person, but even at games she looked irritated, like she'd rather be anywhere else than on the field.

She didn't talk to many people, except Emma. Emma was nice. For a trumpet player. But Sydney didn't strike him as nice, which made him want to poke at her. It had taken a long time, but he'd finally gotten a reaction.

He liked that wink so much he might reconsider his rule against dating a band member. He'd love to get her alone to see if she continued to be this distant and edgy. It was his last season of band, which was almost over, and he'd graduate in the spring. Maybe it was time to lift the ban on band members.

Practice was starting, so Hunter ran to get into place. While they gathered in formation to practice the drill, he couldn't help but smile.

Two hours later, practice ended and his fingers were numb. He should've gone to school somewhere in the South. He looked at the drum line to find Sydney, but he didn't see her face. Then he saw her on the outskirts of the group, edging away. Hunter took a step in her direction.

"Hey, Peters," the drum major called.

Her head snapped up.

"Practice room at two o'clock. We need to run through this again."

Although her jaw clenched, she offered a sharp nod. Then she turned and hustled downfield. Approaching her now wouldn't be smart. He wasn't even sure what he'd say. But he got out of class at two thirty, so maybe he'd wander on down to the practice rooms to bump into her.

"Hey, Hunter," Mike called. He was another tenor, and they sometimes hung out, but Hunter wouldn't call them friends. "You having a party for New Year's again?"

"You know it."

"Can I bring a friend?"

"Don't see why not." Hunter put his sax into the case. "I'll text you details later. I need to talk to my roommate about it."

"Cool. See you Wednesday."

Hours later, Hunter had walked past music practice rooms and had no luck finding Sydney. He checked the time. He was supposed to meet Adam and Free at the comic shop at three thirty. If he didn't head out soon, he'd be late.

He hit the last hallway of practice rooms. It figured the drummers would take the biggest rooms in the farthest building. As he clomped down the stairs, Daniel—not Dan or Danny—the drum major, came out of a room. When no one followed, Hunter thought he'd missed her.

Until a slow beat came from the room where Daniel had left. He stood outside the room and listened for a minute. Then he recognized the tune, the same one he'd played to Sydney this morning. He silently opened the door and entered. She noticed him immediately and shot him a dirty look, but didn't stop playing.

Hunter took a seat at another set of drums and picked up where she played. Her eyes narrowed as she watched him. She picked up the tempo and he followed. She ramped it up again.

Now it just felt like a competition.

He kept up with her—barely. She was good, and he wasn't sure why that kind of surprised him, but it did.

When the song ended, he stood and set the sticks on the stool. "Remind me to never go up against you in any kind of battle. You're relentless."

"You're one to talk."

He smiled. "Seriously. You're good."

"You're not bad yourself. For a reed sucker."

He let the playful insult roll off him. "So what are you pissed off about?"

"Who said I'm pissed?"

"Your face."

"Maybe I just have a resting bitch face."

He laughed. He couldn't help it. She was funny without trying. "Nah. I've seen the resting bitch face." With his index finger he circled the air in front of her head. "This is pissed off. My guess is Daniel said something."

"Daniel's always saying something." She stood and tucked her sticks in her backpack.

Hunter knew he was about to lose her. "Can I ask you a question?"

The corner of her mouth lifted. "You just did."

"Why do you hate band?"

"Because it sucks. It's boring. And I will forever be relegated to playing the cymbals, even though I play as well as, if not better than, at least half the drum line."

Ahhh…now it made sense. Those guys tended to be a little full of themselves. "So why do it?"

"It pays the bills."

"Huh?"

"Scholarship." She hoisted her bag onto her shoulder and headed for the door.

"See you at practice Wednesday?"

"As if I have a choice?"

She sounded so miserable he wanted to cheer her up. "I take requests."

"What?" she asked with her hand on the doorknob.

"You seemed to like 'Let It Go.' I take requests. Something you want to hear?"

She turned and leaned against the door. "Are you saying that if I name a song, you're going to go home and learn it just to play it for me at practice on Wednesday?"

Not exactly. He was thinking more like a song for next week, but she was issuing a challenge. "Sure."

She tilted her head up and narrowed her eyes again as she studied the ceiling for inspiration.

When her gaze returned to his, she smiled wickedly, and he knew he was in trouble.

"'Sweet Child O' Mine.'"

He stared at her.

"Guns N' Roses. See you Wednesday, Tenor." Then she slipped out the door before he could form a response.

He knew the song, but it wasn't one he'd ever considered playing with his sax. His drums? Sure. His guitar? Even better. His night just became full.

He checked his watch. If he sped all the way to the comic shop, he might make it on time. Barely. Catching crap from his friends for being late in order to make real contact with Sydney was well worth it.

When he pulled up at the shop, he was late, so he rushed through the door. Free and Adam were standing at the counter. "Why did I have to come here if we're just talking about the New Year's Eve party? Couldn't we do this at home later?"

"Free has to meet Cary at the gym."

"Then I have rehearsal," Free added.

"Why couldn't it wait? We have, like, a month before the party." He'd avoided this conversation because he had a feeling he knew what it was about.

Free straightened. "We need to talk about invitations. We don't want a repeat of last year."

"Why not? Last year was epic."

Adam crossed his arms. "Your word-of-mouth campaign led to an apartment full of strangers."

"They weren't all strangers."

"Just the entire marching band."

"Not all of the band came, and it was fun." The

drum line missed out, as usual, and only half the brass showed.

"Except for all the drunk bodies laying all over the place the following morning."

Free held up his hands. "I can't say much about that since I don't live with you guys and therefore don't suffer those repercussions, but I agree that it was too crowded to actually have fun with friends."

Adam pointed at Hunter. "And don't forget the catfight that broke out."

"That wasn't my fault. I'm irresistible." In truth, having two girls brawl because they each thought he somehow *belonged* to her hadn't been as cool as it sounded.

If he left it up to Free and Adam, the entire party would consist of the three of them and maybe five other people sitting around sharing a case of beer. His friends needed help and he'd always taken it upon himself to make it happen. In a flash, he knew how to get them to agree to a bigger party.

Hunter's gaze bounced between his friends. "Does that mean you guys are going to have dates this year?"

"Nope," Adam answered, and Free dodged him.

Hunter sighed, even though it was the answer he'd expected. "You guys are pitiful. The epitome of nerds. You get dates, I won't tell everyone and their cousin to come to our party."

He knew the chances of that happening were slim. He'd have his blowout party. Besides, the more people he invited, the greater *their* odds were for hooking up with someone.

"You have a date?" Free asked.

He thought of Sydney, who shouldn't even be in the running. "Not yet. I have plenty of time. Working on some options."

And just like that, Sydney became a real option. He didn't know why he was willing to toss out his no-band-members rule for her, but he knew he wanted a chance.

The door opened behind him and Adam greeted the customer by name, but something about Adam's face made Hunter turn to look. A girl with dark hair stared at them with wide eyes before turning to look at comics. Hunter waved a hand toward the girl.

"What?" Adam whispered.

"Ask her, you idiot. She's cute."

"She's not like that."

Hunter shook his head. Adam needed more help than he'd thought. "Every girl is datable."

Adam didn't respond. At the rate he moved, Hunter had no worries about the size of their party.